Portal of Vaal

Andrew Daly

ISBN-10: 0692450904

ISBN-13: 978-0-692-45090-1

Cover Art by Grace Zhang
Book Design by Lorie DeWorken, Mind the Margins, LLC
Edited by Lorraine Fico-White, Magnifico Manuscripts, LLC

Portal of Vaal is a work of fiction. Names, characters, places, and incidents are the products of the author's imagination or are used fictitiously. Any resemblance to actual events, locales, or persons, living or dead, is entirely coincidental.

TABLE OF CONTENTS

DEDICATIONS

To my parents, who taught me that to search for the light, you'll have to go through a bit of darkness.

To my dog, who taught me that friendship and compassion can come in all shapes and sizes.

To my friends, who taught me that deviating from the normal curve can be acceptable.

To everyone on BossSMP, who taught me that social friendships and bonds aren't necessarily through face-to-face conversations, but can be through a few skillful keystrokes.

To you, who taught me that this was actually worth something to another human being.

Thank you all, and enjoy.

THE BEGINNING

By Andrew Daly

Cold. Autumn evening.
Winter drawing closer with
Every breath the wind takes.
The house on the hill
Holding the inspiration.
Playing my favorite online game,
Minecraft,
In the small green room with the dim
Light and marble-white desktop.

Enjoying the game, I called out,
"This is a great experience!
Why haven't others heard the news?
I must express my emotions about it
For others to feel, somehow!"
I looked across the desktop
For materials to help me achieve my goal.
My wandering eyes eventually settled
On a nearby book.
"This is it!" I exclaimed.
"If books can spread
Faster than nuclear warfare,
And alert the public about new ideas,
Then surely mine will too!"

So I set to work, creating
Characters, plot, conflict,
Stopping only for human
And few society needs.

But oh! The outside was
So tempting with its
Distractions at every turn!
The decisions weighed down,
But I fought back against
Slacking off to achieve
My goal!
Click, click.
Typing, tapping, to tell a tale.
My fingers like miniature cheetahs,
Racing across the track
That was my keyboard.

Sleeping that night
Produced visions of fame,
Fortune, and inspiration
All because of the dream.
And I knew that one day,
It would, and will, come true.
Even to this day, the dream
Has not shown itself yet.

The dream that started
One night, at a
Young boy's house.
The dream of
Portal of Vaal.

The story is now near done;
The last page close to being turned!
I never gave up,
I never fell short,
I kept going until my hand
Was close to falling off.
I know the story will render
Success, so remember, even
If you're working and the
theme park comes to you,
Do NOT ride the coaster.

Chapter 1
THE FOREST

I AWOKE ON A BED OF FLOWERS IN A PRISTINE FOREST. I TRIED remembering how I got there but came up with nothing. Panic almost overtook me, but I struggled not to let my mind be my master. I didn't even know where I was.

I sat up, looked around, and saw some trees, a small grassy path, the flowerbed, the blue sky and perfect white clouds, and a lake in the middle of the clearing. Well, not a lake, but more of a small pond a person could jump into. It seemed to emit something powerful, something almost . . . godlike. I did have a backpack, but it didn't contain much except some sticks and stones. I had only lost my memory, not my wits, so I knew that a few spare rocks and branches couldn't help me very much.

As I lay down to think about what to do, I felt a sharp pain in my back. Grimacing, I felt for the source. It had some kind of handle and was strapped to my back. I drew it out. *Wow . . . I wondered, where could I have gotten this?*

It was a large, shining, diamond sword, the strongest kind of blade known to man, with some blood on it. Hopefully, the blood wasn't mine. But the weapon could come into good use later. Before I lost my memory, I must've been a fighter or something.

I let my mind wander from that subject. I still needed to survive. I started by examining the lake nearby. The water seemed perfectly fine. I bent down to drink and nearly screamed.

Inside the lake, I thought I saw a hideous creature! I then reached out with my sword, as did the creature. I realized it was just a reflection. Was this what I looked like? I had on some kind of shawl, battle armor, and what looked like a monster's face on a side of my head. I poked it. It clearly was not a mask by the pain I experienced in my eye.

The monster sparked my memory. I had a quick vision of it closing in on me. Then, it hissed as its skin puffed outward and—

Thankfully, I jumped back to reality. I decided for now to rest and wait for someone to rescue me. I knew it wouldn't be something a person with a diamond sword would have done, but as far as I knew, I had no skills with it.

After drinking some water and munching on some mushrooms, I fell back to sleep near the lake. *Hopefully*, I thought, *this will all be over soon. I'll be in a warm home and eventually get over this case of amnesia or whatever I have.*

And with that thought in mind, I fell asleep smiling.

Little did I know, I was *horribly* mistaken.

Chapter 2
THE MEETING

FTER THE QUICK NAP, I EXPLORED TO SEE IF THERE WERE ANY signs of civilization. The closest thing I found was the path, but it went on for quite a distance, and I was tired. Getting back to where I woke up earlier, it was already nightfall, and I was still stranded in the forest. Dang it!

I tried to relax in some comfortable bushes but was kept awake with fear. Eventually, trees rustled, even though it was a windless night. No owls or animals could be heard, so I worried.

I grabbed my sword and advanced slowly to the bushes near the dirt path. A girl sprang out of the bushes near me, knocking me over and startling me. I couldn't see her well because it was night but could see her clearly enough to know she wasn't evil.

As any normal person would do, I screamed. The girl seemed startled for a second. I heard some birds in the trees fly off and some rustling in the bushes.

"Quickly, we must hurry! Follow me!" she said as fast as she possibly could. "Wait, but where—"

She snatched my arm, and we ran faster than I thought I could ever run. She sprinted like a cheetah on a sugar rush as trees and landscape zoomed by, but abruptly stopped in a clearing after a few minutes.

Since I was still dizzy from the speed, I continued forward and crashed into a tree. *Smooth move*, I thought to myself. *Embarrass yourself with the first person you've ever met in what you know of your life. Not your best day.*

I noticed her staring at something in either shock, hatred, or both. I looked to see what she was staring at, and nearly ducked, because whatever it was nearly hit me with something.

A bullet? A dart? I checked the tree it hit. The thing was neither, but it *was* an arrow. I looked for the person who shot it and saw a skeleton standing menacingly in the moonlight with a bow and quiver.

I know I didn't have good sight since I crashed into that tree, but trust me, I was seeing straight. The creature was pure bleach white with eye sockets that seemed to stare straight into your soul and steal anything happy belonging there.

For some reason, I got up and ran toward the skeleton, taking my sword out for battle. I had no idea what I was doing. Suicide? It sure seemed like it. The creature's eye sockets seemed to widen in surprise. *You and me both, pal*, I thought.

I stabbed out in front of me, but the skeleton ducked, and my move missed only by an inch. It jumped back like an acrobat, firing a shot straight at my head. I held my sword in front of me, taking the arrow's impact.

I jumped forward, as if I had done this a thousand times before. I made an upward slash from the skeleton's spine, slicing it clean in two and having it disappear into gray dust.

I huffed and bent over, catching my breath. Where the heck

had I learned that? But before I could wonder any more, I heard something behind me. I turned and saw the monster I had seen on my face. It was a shade of green that easily camouflaged into the environment and had a face of torture and grief, with four tiny legs carrying its armless body.

It kept coming closer until it was in front of me. I was paralyzed with fear. It stopped, then hissed, and its skin started to grow outward.

The girl then tackled me to the ground as the creature exploded. The smell of sulfur was overwhelming, and my ears started to ring. She got up, grabbed me, and ran, dragging me wherever her destination was. I didn't even have a chance to say thanks, it happened so fast.

"What are we doing? Where are we going? What the heck was that thing?" I asked.

"We'll discuss everything later."

We? I thought. *And when was later?* She looked in a hurry to get to wherever, so I stayed silent along the rest of the way as I pondered over the hundreds of questions I had accumulated in the past few minutes.

Chapter 3
Monsters 101

After running (or just being a weight for the girl to lug around) for what felt like eternity, I looked up ahead of her and saw she was sprinting to a cottage. It was small and made of wood but it glowed like it had a warm fire inside. I also saw a shadow of a person by the window. This must be who else "we" was.

When the girl and I arrived, she ushered me inside. It was cabin-like, with pictures of her and another girl, this one red-haired, on the fireplace and walls. There was also a small wooden kitchenette and a couch with a log table in front of it facing the fireplace. But there was something weird about the house: one wall had a lever built into it.

That struck me as strange. It was jutting out in the open. I wondered, *Who would leave a lever in plain sight? What does it do, anyway?* But before I could see what it did, a girl grabbed me by the shoulder and turned me to face her. She had long, untied red hair, blue eyes, and wore what looked like a rainbow dress. She was the other girl in the pictures.

"Hej! I'm Furrybunny! But you can call me Furry! Sorry, hej means 'hi' in Swedish! I knew you would come, I just knew you would! Shiro always doubted it." She pointed to the other girl I was with earlier. "But I always believed it! And I was right! Yay!" She started cheering, then skipped out of the room.

I had no idea what just happened, so I went over to "Shiro." Now that we were inside, I could see her better.

She had long brown hair, similar in style to Furry's, had the same blue eyes, and what looked like an exact copy of the rainbow dress. It seemed as if—

"We're sisters? I get that a lot," finished Shiro. "Just friends is really all."

"But how could you—"

"Read your mind?" she asked. "It's pretty simple. Just concentrating in the woods gives you *awesome* powers. Plus, potion-making isn't bad either. Want a sip?" She took out a bottle of red fizzy liquid. I must've wondered what it was in my mind because she instantly responded, "It's fire resistant. Lasts for up to eight minutes!"

"I'm good," I hastily replied because it didn't look too appetizing.

"It's fruit punch flavor," she said.

Trying to change the subject, I refocused to the lever on the wall.

"Oh, that thing," Shiro said. "We'll have to teach you a lesson or two before you go in there."

"Like what?" I asked out of curiosity. I needed permission and training to use a lever? It seemed as though I had come upon the cabin of the Weird Sisters.

"Well . . . oh. Here it is."

Furry came in pushing a giant board like the ones used in

school. Shiro wrote some words on the board with a marker.

"This," she said, "is Monsters 101." She drew and told of skeletons, the bowmen of monsters that I had a not-so-nice encounter with not so long ago. Of zombies, the average minor threat. Of Endermen, in which the title says it all. Of creatures who dwell in another dimension, the Nether. Of Slimes, which were cubes of Jell-O dominating bedrock. Of how to defeat them all by taking advantage of their weak points.

But there was one monster that *really* caught my attention.

Shiro drew a block on a tall, slim body with four legs and colored the creature green. It was exactly like the monster I saw when I looked in the lake, and the one that almost killed me earlier with an explosion.

"This," Furry said, "is a—"

"Creeper!" I shouted. It just came into my head quickly, and I blurted it out. We all sat there in silence.

Finally, Furry spoke. "That's ... right. No one usually knows what it is that quick." She turned to Shiro. "He's ready."

They both stood up.

"Okay," Shiro said, "you're ready for the final exam."

I didn't like the way she smiled when she said "exam." Furry went over to the wall and pulled the switch I saw earlier. The wall next to it instantly opened up into what looked like a mix between a security center and an announcer's booth. It had a section of glass dividing the fancy electronics and the other side of the room, where there was only a trapdoor.

"First," she said, "stand on the trapdoor."

I did as I was told.

Shiro then glanced at a screen and said, "Activating in three ... two ... one ... now!" She pulled a lever.

I grimaced and waited for the worst. Nothing happened.

"Hey, can you help me with this?" Shiro asked.

I hesitated, then Furry came up and said, "I'll take your spot. If nothing's on it, sometimes it blows up."

I didn't particularly like that picture, so I nodded and went over to pull the lever. It slid like a charm. How could she have had trouble operating it?

Just then, the trapdoor opened under Furry, and she fell into the hole, screaming all the way down. For some reason, my "suicide instincts" kicked in, and I jumped down the hole after her.

I didn't like how my first day was turning out so far.

Chapter 4
FINAL EXAM

I FELL DOWN FOR... WELL, I DIDN'T HAVE A WATCH TO CHECK, but I fell down for what seemed like a long time. I thought I saw ground below me after a few minutes, so I readied for the worst. But I didn't hear a splat, just a splash, and water splashed around me. I looked down.

I had landed in some water that had cushioned my fall. There wasn't much to see though, since it was dark. The only things I could recognize were the water I was standing in and a stone wall right behind me. I heard a sound that made chills run down my spine. It was a moan. A *deathly* moan.

I slowly and carefully turned around to see a green figure that smelled like a dead rat, with a blue shirt and blue jeans wading through the water after me. It probably didn't take a genius to figure out that there was a zombie chasing after me. I heard some sort of creak from a different section of the darkness. *Another skeleton?* I thought. I heard more moans and creaks and hissing emanating from all around.

I realized Furry and Shiro had thrown me into a monster

spawner, which is basically a dungeon to store monsters. Then I realized something that made me sick. This kind was for battling them!

Well, it all made sense now. The stone walls, the water, the lack of light, the way Shiro had said final "exam." How could I have *not* seen that coming? Well, one thing was for sure. I had to go rescue Furry. Who knows what could have been happening as I was being chased down? I didn't even want to think of the possibilities.

My strength was instantly driven by my desire to . . . I have no idea. Basically, suicide instincts again. I pulled my sword out of the scabbard on my back and approached the nearest zombie. It was holding out its arms, like it wanted to hug my delicious, juicy brain.

"Hug this!" I yelled, as I brought my sword down and through the zombie's head, body, and all the way down to its knees where it exploded into nonexistence.

I heard something whizzing through the air near me, then brought my sword around to deflect nine skeletons' arrows. I was intimidated at first, but courage kicked in. Since they surrounded me, I brought both my hands to the hilt and spun around. My sword slashed through their bodies, where there were four, three, two, one, none left. I stood there, panting.

But the fight wasn't over yet. Once I heard the hiss behind me, I instinctively threw my hands behind my back, grabbed both sides of the creeper's head, and flipped it, back and forth, across the cold, hard floor. I slammed it one last time in front of me, and it disappeared into a stream of vapor like the skeleton I had killed near the lake.

Exhausted and sweating like a fire hydrant, I looked around in the darkness. There were strange yellow-green orbs floating where the monsters once stood. Threatened and afraid, I approached them slowly until I could reach the spheres. I stuck my hand out near one, and it flew into me. I wanted to scream, but I heard (and you're gonna think I'm crazy) it whisper to me.

It spoke in a light, airy voice. *Let me heal you,* it said. *You need me. I won't hurt you.*

Even though every atom in my body was telling me to keep my guard up, I started to relax. The orb flew into my skin, feeling hot at first. Then it felt warm and comforting. Soon they all flew into me, refilling me with strength.

I heard the moan again and realized that the monsters were coming back to life in the darkness. I needed to escape—and fast. I wandered aimlessly until I saw an area where the water went down into a hole. I started to have second thoughts, but the voice whispered, *Go.* I jumped down like before, except it wasn't as long of a jump as last time.

I fell, landing on my butt.

Nice move, the voice whispered. At this point, I wasn't really sure if I should trust the weird whisper anymore.

I ignored it, stood up, and saw that I was in a giant cave with light coming from a pool of lava. Not too far away sat a giant . . . Jell-O? Wait, no. I saw a giant, hideous, oozing green Slime, with huge, blobby eyes and a mouth the size of half a door. It looked a lot like Jell-O, though, but I was *not* going to eat it.

I realized it wasn't entirely transparent. There was a weird shape where—oh no! This wasn't good. In the center, there was a human-shaped figure, with long red hair and—

Oh crap! "Furry!" I yelled, trying to get her attention. I also realized something else frightening. The Slime was asleep when I came in, and that's why it didn't immediately attack me. But because of my scream, I saw a blobby eye open in anger and frustration. And another. And then, its mouth let out a hideous, loud, evil scream. Oops.

It started jumping toward me. I had no idea how it did that, considering I can barely even walk after I wake up.

Anyway, the battle. The unholy creature was hopping around, chasing after me, and it was some time until I used common sense and drew out my sword. I turned around to face it, but I tripped on a rock, falling flat on my butt and watched my sword fly up in the air, its point falling toward my chest. I slid backward on all fours while the Slime jumped in front of where I had just been as the sword fell. It hit the monster in the face, causing it to roar in pain.

"Take that, you oversized mountain of Jell-O!" I yelled so loudly, so that even Shiro might have heard it. The Slime started to ooze away, but not entirely.

The rest of it turned into three smaller Slimes. I'm not the best at math, but I'm pretty sure diamond sword to the face plus Slime equals one big dead monster, not three more Slimes. I tried striking them again, but they turned into even more Slimes. I knew that I could've instantly grabbed Furry and ran, but I wanted to make sure that fiend knew to stay away. Besides, I didn't see any discernible exit.

I kept getting chased by them, and then I saw the lava pit. I tried picking one Slime up to throw it in there, but it landed on my head and started to ooze what must've been acid. It immediately felt like my head was melting, so I tossed it back off. Apparently, I had to lure them over there. Then I remembered my backpack.

I fished out a stick and tossed it into the lava. About five went after it, playing catch, and followed it into the burning liquid. They didn't melt, but I figured it would hold them off for a bit. I drew my sword back out and looked at the remaining Slimes. They weren't that big, but they were plentiful. I tried hitting the smallest one. I sliced it in half, and when it oozed away, it all disappeared.

I smiled at the thought of what I could do next. I pointed my sword downward and it stood up on its blade. I hopped onto the cross and started jumping. Pretty soon, I had my own diamond sword pogo stick, and it was vanquishing Slimes like crazy. It was all over in a minute or two. I looked around for any missed monsters, but luckily, there were none. I looked over and ran to help Furry. She was covered in slime, and she looked like she was passed out. But there was something strange that glinted in the lava's light when I came closer.

"Hej! What took you so long?" She instantly stood up, and she was wearing a full set of diamond armor. As a reaction, I screamed, jumped back, and tripped backward over a rock. Again.

"You took forever," she said with a grin.

"Where did . . . how did you . . ." I started to ask, but I was completely tongue-tied.

"Well, I have to say, you passed," Furry said. "The final exam was to go in and rescue me. And you did that," she checked a clock in her bag, "in forty-five minutes. Good work!" She climbed up a ladder in the corner that I didn't even see before.

I stood there, thinking, *They definitely are crazy. But hey, it works.*

"Coming?" Furry asked down.

I gathered up my thoughts and looked up. "Coming!" I said, and climbed up the ladder to light.

Chapter 5
THE LEGEND

AFTER I CAME OUT OF THE MONSTER SPAWNER, I IMMEDIATELY jumped outside and ran around, joyful that I was still alive and now in fresh air. But I could only run around so much after killing dozens of monsters without getting tired. When I came back in, Shiro and Furry greeted me with a "Congratulations" and a shove over to some bookshelves.

"What is this?" I asked. There was some sort of strange black table, with red and blue cloths draped over it. But the weird part was the floating book that followed my eyes, and the strange figures leaping off the bookshelves right into the open book.

"This is an enchanter," Furry said. "Just put your sword on it and you'll see."

"Okay," I said, trying to be more careful after they had sent me into the tortured pit of darkness. Shiro read my mind again.

"Just do it, the book won't bite," she said.

I decided to try not to be a wimp in front of them, so I took out my sword and placed it on the strange table.

The blank book filled with mysterious figures I had never seen before. It also showed the orbs I had collected earlier and random numbers for each line of figures. The voice whispered inside me again. *Pick any spell you like. You will lose some part of me, but I will never leave you.* I was getting ready to call the cops on this thing.

I looked at some pages before I found a spell that seemed interesting. I glanced at the figures and orbs, wondering what they could mean.

Tap it, the voice said.

I tapped the line of text. The orbs came off the page and burst into my sword with a bright flash of light. When the light faded, I curiously and cautiously picked up my sword, almost dropping it as the tip burst into flames. I thought it was on fire, but the flames died down almost instantly. I turned to Shiro and Furry, who were still staring at me.

"What the heck just happened?" I asked, shocked by . . . well, what the heck had just happened.

"That," Shiro said, "was an enchantment. And it looks like you got Fire Aspect II. Nice one."

I must have looked confused because Furry jumped in and said, "Sometimes, it allows you to kill monsters with fire. Just slash them with it, and they burst into flames."

The concept sounded pretty cool to me. I went outside and tried it on some monsters in a nearby cave. It worked, although I remember they didn't like it too much when I set them burning into nearby giant pits.

When I came back inside, they wanted to get me a cake for finishing Monsters 101, and they needed to know my name. How they went so long without knowing my name, I have no idea.

"Uh . . ." Since I still didn't have my memory, I didn't know my name. Unfortunately, Shiro chose that moment to read my mind. "You don't even know your own name, and you just randomly woke up in my part of the woods?" she asked. "Well, yeah, I guess," I said, not knowing whether to disagree or agree. Fact was fact. Furry's face lit up like a flashlight.

"Well, that's perfect!" Furry said, with an enthusiastic smile.

"You're kidding, right?" I asked, but she actually sounded serious.

"No," she said. "This is just what the legend told of!"

"Furry!" Shiro said through gritted teeth. Furry's smile suddenly was replaced by a look of disappointment.

"Sorry," she said, in a quiet voice.

I was about to ask a question, but then Shiro quickly said, "We'lldiscussallthis tomorrow!" and took off to another part of the house. I looked over to Furry.

She glanced at me and said, "She gets a little touchy on the subject. Just give her some time. "'Night"

"'Night," I said, not knowing what else to say. I went to the living room to sleep on the couch, easily falling asleep to the crackling fire in the burning hearth and the sound of crickets chirping their songs outside. At least they knew what to do in their lives.

The next morning, I felt wide awake and ready to go at any monster that got in my way. The only sound, though, was a knock on the door. But before I even got up to walk to the entrance, Shiro passed me and opened the door. I went to see who Shiro had just let in.

A strikingly handsome man with black, spiky hair in a white button-down shirt and perfect-fitting jeans stood at the entrance. If you mashed up the three most popular movie stars, they would look like an average person next to him. I could see why Shiro got to the door before I did, but she didn't seem to see this handsome stranger walking up to her house as odd or even interesting.

"Hej Neon," she said nonchalantly. Furry came out of the bedroom and walked up behind Shiro.

"Hey, Shiro. Furry. And . . . who's that?" He stared in my direction. She whispered something in his ear. His eyes widened.

"I see," he said. "Come on, Ida would really want to meet him." He pronounced the strange name like *ee-duh*.

Who the heck was Ida? I wondered. But Shiro seemed into the conversation once this "Neon" mentioned "Ida," and she didn't seem to be paying attention to my thoughts. I could probably think freely. *And what was up with her whispering? They should at least have told me.* Furry tapped my shoulder.

"Come on, we're leaving," she said. I looked ahead and saw that Neon and Shiro had already run outside.

"Oh, gotcha!" I said, following her out of the house. Neon and Shiro were waiting at a beach, both in small boats.

"Come on, let's go!" Neon shouted, shoving me a boat with some small oars I thought were waffle irons at first. I caught it, then set it in the water, and shoved off to . . . well, wherever we were all going. Out of curiosity, I asked where we were going.

Furry was about to say something, but Shiro instantly turned around and cast a hard glare at her like the night before. Furry stayed quiet. Nobody said anything. I just rowed with the small oars Neon had given me.

On the way there, we saw a small group of squid. Furry looked down and stared at them. I think my eyes were playing tricks on me because I saw the squid nod and swim out of the way. The ride returned to the same boring and quiet travel it was when we started, although faster for some reason.

About an hour later I was half asleep from boredom, not paying attention to where I was going. My boat hit the land so hard I flew out and did a face-plant into the ground. Luckily, no one was looking or laughed. We got out of the boats and onto the land, where I saw an enormous castle and looked up in awe.

"Yep," Neon said. "That's Ida's castle all right."

It was made entirely of the finest stone, built in the shape of a tall and slim archer-tower style, with a big set of double-doors, soon pulled aside by the two wolves guarding it. As we walked throughout the grand hallway's luxurious atmosphere on its thick and woolen carpet, there were wolves everywhere. Wolves with food on trays on their heads, wolves carrying scrolls in a pouch, wolves with saddles.

Wait—with saddles?

I started to turn to not let them take me, but one wolf slipped right under me and got my feet in the harnesses. The rest got Shiro, Furry, and Neon and we headed atop the wolves up the stairs to the outside entrance of what seemed to be a throne room.

Only the wolves Neon and I were riding continued into the throne room, where they let us off, and ran off to get back to their work, shutting the door behind them.

I looked around the grand room filled with rare jewels and expensive pieces of highly polished armor. Near the throne, a picture of a young woman wearing one of the sets of armor was displayed in a nearby case. It looked a little used. Okay, it looked like it was used so much that it was only brand new in the prehistoric eras.

Just behind the fine stone and velvet throne, two wolves rushed in, escorting the woman from the picture onto the throne. The wolves sat beside the throne. The "queen," apparently, was a tall woman with wavy blond hair . . . in a batman costume? She had a long black cape and a wolf in her lap. Her other features were hidden behind her mask.

"Hello," she said, her voice like a gentle breeze. "Oh, hej Neon. Is this him?" She pointed to me.

"Yes, Ida," he said. "He is the one who appeared by the lake, with no memory."

"Interesting. Very interesting. So you don't even know your own *name*?"

I shook my head.

She sighed. For what reason, I have no idea.

"It was told in the legend that you would come. That you would destroy all of this evil."

Destroy all evil? I barely had enough sense to get out of a monster spawner alive.

"Sorry, I have no idea what you're talking about. What legend?" I asked. That was the first time I heard of me being at least somewhat important. But a legend? I must've lost more past than I thought.

"Here is the story," Ida began. "A long time ago, about the twenty-second century, on an average day, certain people invaded the world. Dead, evil ones that had been put to death for their crimes. They had come back for revenge and have now already taken over most of our lands. We call them the Dark Ones now. There was only one hope. That hope was The Knights of Archlinder."

"The what of who now?" I asked, hoping to get something out of this.

"Just wait until the story is finished!" Ida said angrily.

"The Knights of Archlinder was thought up by a philosopher who believed that if something bad happened, we could always rely on Archlinder, the creator of everything you see right now. Eventually, it did work for him, but others thought he was crazy and denied his ways. However, once the Dark Ones came, everyone tried to fight back on their own, soon realizing they had no chance. The few that survived got together and followed the philosopher's ways. They united to become the Knights of Archlinder, each relying on one another to save the world and take it back from the cold, dead hands of the returned."

We stood there in silence, absorbing the story. "So, why am I here, then?" I asked, very curious. How did all of this even connect with me?

"Because," Ida said, "the legend also told of a hero who would finally eliminate the darkness. This hero would wake up by the lake, with no memories of his past. That was Shiro's lake."

I suddenly remembered waking up on the bed of flowers. "So . . . can you help me get my memory back?"

"That is not relevant at the moment," Ida said. "You must go undercover and join the Knights of Archlinder. That is what the prophecies have foretold. In fact, the prophecy is right here."

She patted her wolf on the back, started petting it, and then lightly touched it on the spine. The wolf pup's eyes glowed red, vapor flowed out of its mouth, and it spoke in a dark and ominous voice.

"*The hero to kill darkness will rise from the lake. With no memories, they shall awake. They will be a Knight of Archlinder and rise above all. For they to decide, the world be prospered or fall.*" The wolf pup returned to his normal state and started licking Ida. She put the pup down, and the three wolves returned behind the throne.

"So now you see why this is so important," she said.

"Why did that wolf pup just talk?" I asked.

"It was a pup from a family of oracle wolves. Now you understand what you must do, correct?"

"Understood," I said, trying to look as serious as possible. I was still trying to absorb what she had just told me.

"You will spend the next few days training with Neon," she looked down at Neon, "and traveling to the academy by foot."

"Why not by boat?" I said. Last time I went to a place by foot, I nearly blew up.

"It is landlocked. Plus, it has a few special features." Ida looked the way Shiro did when she said "final exam." I didn't like where this was heading.

"Now, you are dismissed," Ida said, the wolves ushering us out.

"Wait," I said. Ida tilted her head, as if to say, "Go on."

"Do you possibly know what my name is?"

She hesitated .With some difficulty, she replied, "Your name is Motorthud. Now, you may leave." She turned back around, the now-closed doors separating us.

What was she trying to hide?

The wolves once again put us on their backs and led us out through the throne room with Shiro and Furry and left us outside the castle.

"Well, that was strange," I told Neon.

"You're telling me," he said. "I live here, and that wasn't even normal for my standards."

We got back in the boats and left to train in the forest per Ida's instructions. I thought of my new name, Motorthud. It was strange, but as most say, the name makes the person. Or, according to Ida, the hero.

Chapter 6
READINESS IS KEY

I SPENT THE NEXT WEEK TRAINING AND LEARNING AS MUCH AS I could about what I needed to know to get into the Academy of the Knights of Archlinder. Neon helped me practice my sword skills by battling him and some wooden dummies he set up in the forest. It seemed impossible to beat Neon at first, but once I battled him a few more times, I learned his style and soon tied him in a match.

For archery, Shiro helped by carving figures into trees and having me shoot at them. Once she told me to keep my eye on the target and my hand steady, I was a pro in no time. As for tests and history, Ida said that few knew that kind of stuff anyway, so I didn't need to study it.

For disguises, Furry was a great tutor. After succeeding in finding Waldo a few times, I could pick out a man in a crowd from three miles away. She also taught me Morse code, and a bit of what to wear as a disguise depending on certain places. There were, however, a few choice things I needed to know overall.

"You've gotta say 'Oh my Arch!' when something amazing or something you didn't see coming happens," Furry said. "And if anyone asks, you're from another part of Vaal."

"Vaal?" I asked.

"Vaalbara. It's where you are, what these lands are called. My Arch, you *really* have no memory."

I smiled at the joke. I was tense, but it made me lighten up for the challenge ahead. But the thing she said next made me a little uncomfortable.

"And never, ever, ever, ever, *ever* say anything at *all* about me, Shiro, or Ida."

"Why can't I?"

"Well, because . . ." She never finished her sentence because Neon showed up at the door. That meant it was time to go off to the Academy. Shiro came in, we all said our farewells, and Neon and I left the forest.

Neon told me to pack light but with enough food to last us for a day or two. He said I could also bring a memento along with my weapon, so I pondered about that. I decided to bring a flower from Shiro's forest and a wristband from Furry in case I got "homesick." Before, they were just kind strangers. But now, to me, they were family.

I sighed, not knowing when, or even if, I would see them again. Since Ida said I was a hero sent to kill darkness, that meant I probably had to make some sacrifices. Would one of them be my life? I instantly shook away the thought. After all, Neon said for survival training, I had to keep focusing on the positive, or I would starve, slow down, and be eaten. He didn't really help with that example.

But a few hours into the journey, I had a question on my mind that was bugging me.

"Neon?" I asked.

"Yeah?" He kept walking with his eyes straight ahead, focused on the Academy.

"Why are you coming to the Academy with me?"

He instantly stopped and turned to face me. "Motorthud, I know you have no memory, but hopefully you still know what it means to serve your lands. Even though they are against my friends, joining the Knights is the least I can do to help all of us. I join the Knights and I slay the Dark Ones. That means they also stay away from the forest. It is right on the edge of our lands' protection. If we lose the smallest bit of it, Shiro, Ida, Furry, and everything living there will be as good as dead since they will be in the Dark Ones' territory."

I couldn't see all of his face since he turned away, but I think I saw some tears about to fall. It was then I realized that he must be really passionate about Ida. Whatever possible reality he was thinking, I wanted to keep it from happening as well.

He tried to change the subject. "It looks like the sun's going down. We should probably set up camp soon."

Setting up camp and resting sounded good to me. I could've used some sleep. Unfortunately though, I had to nearly break my back to set up the tent on the mountain ledge. I also nearly fell hundreds of feet into a gorge when extending the tent line but Neon quickly grabbed my hand and pulled me back to the top before I could do so.

When Neon was about to take first shift and I was about to head off to sleep, we heard a rustle in the bushes. We instinctively pulled out our swords and waited for the monster to come out. All that came out, however, was a pig. We looked at each other, then back at the pig. We both smiled.

We had roasted pork chops for dinner that night. The

rest of the night was uneventful. I woke up in the morning to find Neon fast asleep on his backpack. I just couldn't resist. I grabbed a nearby chicken, held it to his face, and then squeezed the chicken. It squawked so loudly, he woke up with his hands pressed against his ears.

"Next time," I said, putting the chicken down, "I take first watch."

"There won't be a next time," he said. "We're almost there!" I looked to the east. He was right. The Academy seemed like a few hills away.

Along the way, there was only one thing we encountered that was strange. We found a person who was doubled over, wore a cloak, looking hurt, and appeared to be on the way up the mountain. I drew close to see if I could help.

"Stay at a distance, Motorthud," Neon warned me.

I did. I asked, "Sir? Are you okay—"

"*Ssscccrrreee!*" the man yelled. The cloaked figure transformed into what looked like a shadowy phoenix with midnight black feathers and fiery talons. I ran backward and nearly stumbled over a rock. Then I remembered, *I have a sword.* I unsheathed it, and its fire aspect caused it to blaze with glory.

"Time to reheat this chicken," I said. "This time it'll be sliced, diced, and burnt!" I rushed near the creature on the balls of my feet, the sword carrying me to the monster until the sword embedded into the monster's shadow-black foliage. It let out another horrible screech and hovered toward me, shooting out feathers like a porcupine shoots out quills. Most I dodged, but one landed right in my shoulder, feeling like a small knife.

I jumped close again and sliced into the cut I had put in earlier, but the creature let loose one last screech and exploded into shadow-colored smoke.

"What was that?" I asked, panting from nervousness and fright.

"That was your first Dark One," he responded, somewhat smiling. "I'm proud of you. Anyway, they're usually that black color with a purple kind of flow, appearing in forms of all different kinds of animals and other evil forms." He shuddered. "Although, not all of them are that easy."

Neon put a midnight feather from the Dark One into his bag. "Now come on, the Academy's just up the hill, and it's almost time for lunch. We don't have time to waste."

I agreed, also feeling the feather in my arm getting more painful.

Neon and I ran up the hill as fast as we could until we reached the top at noon. I was huffing and puffing. Then, the world started to spin. Neon sounded far off, and I couldn't make out what he was saying. I fell, and then the world turned black before my eyes.

Chapter 7
A HARSH WELCOME

I WAS GREETED BY THE FACES OF THREE UNKNOWN PEOPLE IN A room with harsh light. However, Neon wasn't one of them. "Neon . . ." I groaned.

"Relax. He's in a better place now." I looked up to see a person in a green cloak, with a detailed face and blond hair, hidden under a green sleeping cap without a pom-pom.

"You mean he's dead?!" I sprang up, suddenly wide awake now.

"What? Heck no, he's just packing up his stuff in the dorm."

"Oh, okay," I said with relief.

"However, it looks like you fainted pretty hard there," he said, pulling out what looked like two irons. "Your heart might need some reviving." He rubbed the two irons together. "And . . . clear—"

"No, no, no!" I said, holding the irons away from me. "I'm good. Thanks."

"Well, I say you have a few nasty cuts. I'll be back with some disinfectant." He left the room, leaving me with the two strangers. The first one was a cloaked figure with a cloak like mine and glowing red eyes. His face was mostly hidden under the shadow of his hood, which extended into a light gray robe down to his feet. The other could best be described as round. He had a large stomach and a blond bowl haircut. He also wore a heavy, brown wolfskin coat.

"So . . . who are you guys?" I asked, trying not to be suspicious for Furry's sake. She seemed like a good person to trust, after providing me with food and housing. The first person, the one with the red eyes, spoke.

"I'm Yoshpog. But everyone calls me Yosh. I joined the Academy to serve my lands." He held his arm to his heart and looked into the distance, acting as if it deserved a live audience and applause.

"Okay," I said. *Serve my lands,* I thought. *That's why Neon said he was joining, too. I wonder if they ever met.* The second person, the one in the brown, now spoke. "Hey! I'm Omalic! I joined the Academy to . . . wait, why did I join? Ah well, we can discuss that later. So, who are you?"

I almost struggled to remember my own name. But I couldn't forget because Furry once said that names have power. Or was it Ida? Shiro? There were so many people I was still getting used to.

"I'm Motorthud."

Yosh made a skeptical face. "No, that's a bit too long of a name. We could get you a nickname. How about—"

"Thud?" Omalic interrupted into Yosh's thoughts. "Nice to meet you, then!"

"No. Hmm . . . Motor works," he said, snapping his fingers together as the idea formed.

"Oh," Omalic said disappointedly.

"By the way," I said, remembering something. "Omalic, right? Who was the other person . . . the doctor?"

"Oh, that mental patient?" Yosh asked. "That's Sonicar, though everyone calls him Sonic."

Just then, Sonic happened to walk back in the room. "It turns out your fainting was an allergic reaction caused by you running all the way here and suffering physical exhaustion."

"English, please?" Omalic asked.

Sonic sighed, then explained, "Feather caused sneezies plus tired equals pass out."

"Oooohhh," we said.

"So can I go to the Academy now?" I asked.

"Sure," Sonic answered, "but be sure to—"

We didn't hear the rest because we had already run out of the hospital wing.

"Dang kids!" he yelled.

◆　　◆　　◆

The Academy looked amazing. The main building had what seemed to be a giant sword running downward through it, but we explored the outside first. There was an archery range, treehouse, a huge forest, sparring arena, pool, and the hospital wing we already visited. It had everything anyone could ask for.

Then we all explored inside. There was a grand library with interestingly themed books from swordsmanship to disguise. The next floor had our dorms for all the knights. Counting every dorm bed, there were sixteen of us excluding teachers. We saw the classrooms and our dorm room. But strangely, we couldn't find anyone. Until we came to the cafeteria.

The cafeteria was on the fourth floor, which also happened to be the Academy roof. There was a large group sitting at the tables, listening to some man at a podium making an announcement. When Omalic, Yosh, and I walked in, the man stopped speaking. He wore a gold tinted helmet and had a biker jacket and purple eyes. He turned to face us, along with the rest of the full cafeteria.

He seemed surprised for a moment, then recovered. "Knights and Dukes of Archlinder," he proclaimed, "please welcome our new student . . . "

"Motorthud," I replied. Almost everyone applauded. There was one person who looked angry. I could tell he hated me before we even met. After that though, the announcer said the meeting was over and we could all get up and meet each other.

I spoke to all of the knights. There were sixteen in all and I had trouble memorizing their names except for the one that despised me, Major. When we shook hands, he nearly crushed mine, doing it with a sneer on his face.

I also met the teachers: Allitode for history, Bluewolf for swordsmanship, Loi for secrecy and disguise, and Kardon for archery. The man who asked who I was happened to be Acyberpoet, also known as Acy. He was also the vice president of the Academy, so I had to be pretty careful around him. However, there was no main principal, which struck me as odd. When asking around as to why, nobody could provide a definitive answer. However, Neon, Omalic, Yosh, and I were tired, so we headed off to our dorm. It was nice.

It had a planter with mushrooms, four regular beds, bookshelves, some paintings, a storage chest, a music box, and Yosh's Chicago Creepers poster, which was a poster of a sports team for some random sport called *spleef.* We all collapsed into our beds, and I fell asleep smiling.

Yep, I thought. *I'm going to like it here at the Academy.*

Chapter 8
JUST A REGULAR SCHOOL DAY

THE DAY STARTED OFF ON A STRANGE NOTE: WAKING UP TO THE smell of a chicken. My eyes popped open to see Neon holding a chicken nearly a foot from my face. I tumbled out of my bed toward him, which caused him to fall and the chicken to plop onto his face.

"Nice try," I said, "but you're gonna have to get up earlier to fool me." I walked over to the bedside table and checked my schedule. I had history, swords, lunch, archery, and secrecy. However, I did have time after classes to practice swimming and sparring or just to read a good book in the library.

I headed upstairs to Allitode's class, where the entrance was surrounded by a variety of levers and switches. The inside was a bit more inviting. The walls had ores, photos of Allitode at vacation spots, a few random trinkets, vials of no real interest, and a music player chained up near the back of the room with a sign stating, "DO NOT PLAY THAT DISC." I made a mental note to not sit near the back of the room.

In the front of the room, there was a large white podium

with lights built into the front. I was early, so it was a few minutes before everyone came in the class. Then, Allitode walked into the room.

He had slick, black, combed-over hair and wore a tuxedo with a rose and hankie in the shirt pocket (fancy!), and a white eye mask on top of a handsome, yet near expressionless, face. He looked like a regular who you would see at an opera. He discussed with the class the War of 2026 and how to protect ourselves if the Dark Ones ever came. It was fun, though. After reading the section, he let us admire his collection of vials and bottles. One student, Buzzy, started juggling them without dropping one. Leon appeared to be at the top of the class when Allitode asked the required questions. He wasn't a nerd, but he seemed like a genius, I can assure you. Poey seemed to like Allitode as much as I did, since he left a box of fancy eggs on the podium when he came in. But soon the bell rang, and I was off to swordsmanship.

The lesson was taught by Swords Teacher Bluewolf, as everyone called him. He started roll call almost immediately after everyone entered the classroom. He had a stern look on his face and started the lesson with the following pep talk:

"So you maggots think you can stand a chance against the Dark Ones? Ha! I think a pig could do better! I'm here to train you in the art of swords and other weapons and will whip you all into better shape. Who wants to come up to the board to show what happens when you hold your sword the wrong way in an explosion?"

Not the best lesson ever. But then, the actual swordsmanship began in the sparring arena, a giant cage match of bloodshed. Or at least, it would have been, if not for the strict "no killing" policy. When we were sparring I had to practice against Major and since Blue told me to always sum up your opponent, I did. I judged his white hood and robe, his cast-gold sword, his gray sleeves, and his slime-like face. No really, he looked like the Slime I fought back in the spawner. We both ran at each other, unsheathing our swords for battle. My diamond swept against his gold blade and the battle had begun.

Although I have a talent for swords, I didn't have any armor because Blue said that was for rookies or higher, not "newbies." Great. After our swords clashed I jumped back as he lunged for my shoulder. I felt the strength of his sword striking down. Was he insane? Was he actually trying to *kill* me? I saw something in his eyes that made me confirm, *yes.*

As he struck down again with his golden death, I did a backflip in an arc, landing in a lunging position behind where his sword struck the ground. He rushed at me again, so I threw myself to the right, dodging his attack, but he kept going right into the cage. His helmet only made it worse for him, vibrating every which way, confusing him. This was my chance.

I charged forward, sword held straight out in front of my body, heading for the armor at the small of his back. By the time he gathered his senses, I was only a foot away. The sword, without any command from me, suddenly ignited. I tried to stop it, but it was no use. The diamond sword, blazing, impaled itself into the chest plate of Major's armor. Still blazing, the sword actually *melted* the armor onto Major. He already looked semi-conscious, but now, he was instantly knocked out, possibly with serious burns.

"Tigs, Cooster!" Blue shouted, "Get Major to Sonic! I'll deal with the know-it-all." Cooster and Tigs got a stretcher and hurried Major to the hospital wing, thankfully only mere yards from the cage. Bluewolf walked up to me with an angry look on his face. I was not looking forward to what he would say next. But he didn't scream at me or yell his lungs out or utter a forceful command. He just growled, "Acyberpoet's office. Now."

I was shocked. Not at the lack of volume, but at the punishment. First day of school, and I'm already in the VP's office? So much for a hero.

He led me to a cave entrance under the school, which was guarded by a gate so that no one could sneak in. He pressed a button and turned a key on his key ring, opening the gate. He ushered me inside then went back out, shutting me in behind him.

Okay, so I admit that melting a student's armor isn't the best thing to do, but if you know swords, you can't control their power. Sometimes, they can be free horses. Strong, wild, and willing to help. But other times, they can be like bulls. Strong, wild, and extremely random, with a hatred for anything that gets in its way. My sword was—well, I guess that one's a bit obvious.

I gazed around the cave Bluewolf had led me into. It had . . . as all caves have, nothing really interesting. Only some rocks and—wait. There was one wall that had a door built into it, with a sign that read:

Acyberpoet's Office
It's your fault for being here.

Otherwise, everything else was intact. I felt like complaining that the accident wasn't my fault, but how is complaining to a sign even heroic or even *socially acceptable?* I walked in through the door, expecting it to be damp, smelly, and rat-infested. However, the VP's room was calming and clean. It had a dark green carpet, a bulletin board with memos from Chinese takeout menus to a grocery list, a wolf in the corner of the room, a furnace heater, some bookshelves, an overhead lamp, and

Acy himself. He wasn't doing anything and didn't really make me nervous, even with his tough biker appearance. His smile made me forget any bad aspects of him.

"Don't be afraid. Come in, have a seat." He indicated the seat directly in front of him. I, a bit cautiously, sat down. You don't exactly expect a nice welcome from a vice principal, especially if it's your first day and you're in his office. "Now I heard about your little incident with Majo—"

"I can explain! My sword . . . it just . . . y'know . . . and . . ."

"Now, calm down," he said. "I know what happened out there, and I understand."

How could he know? "You do?" I wasn't really sure how a vice principal would know about this kind of situation, but I didn't interrupt.

"Yes, I understand. Because I was in your position once. Back when I was at this Academy, my sword had Sharpness II, and when sparring with Allitode, your teacher, it activated and he had to get dozens of stitches on his face."

That explains why he had that mask, I thought.

"And then the other vice principal at the time put me in detention for days, saying it was my fault for hurting Allitode so badly. And I don't want the same to happen to another student—ever." He got up from his desk and walked around the room. "But I know Bluewolf. He wouldn't let you go free from consequences, even if you were a war hero."

The happiness and hope once in me drained away when he said that.

"But, if we don't tell him," he glanced over at me, "he won't be the slightest bit angry, and everything will be normal again."

"But how is he going to know if I'm just walking around the campus in clear sight?"

Acy then grinned, maybe smirked? "Well, you are going to have to stay in here."

"What?" I exclaimed.

"But," Acy continued, "while I am off—thankfully I'm going to have to walk around classes today—you can stay in my office. And if you're missing social interaction, then . . ." Acy pressed a switch on his desk, where the bulletin board slid up to reveal a bunch of closed-circuit cameras' screens. They showed every location in the school—the hospital, the classes, the cafeteria, and even in the pool.

"Well, you can have fun with that. I'll just be heading out to lunch. What would you like to eat?"

◆   ◆   ◆

I spent most of the day spying on some of my dorm mates and observing the classes I had to miss for detention. I felt that it was possibly inadequate for a student almost killing another to not only miss punishment, but to get preferential treatment, but what do I know? The education system has been messed up for centuries.

A couple of hours later, Acy came back and said I was free. I spent the rest of the day after that sparring with some people I didn't know that well, like Geo, Lewis, and Riccardo. After three rounds with each, I went for a swim. The pool's surface was sparkling and you could clearly see the bottom, but it was still deep. When the water hit your face you instantly felt revived. After an hour or two of swimming and doing laps, it was time for lights out. I thought I *was* in major trouble, but it turned out to be a pretty good day. After all, the first day is usually the best, right?

Chapter 9
Into the Woods!

THE REST OF THE WEEK WENT ALONG AS MY FIRST DAY DID, minus the freak accident and getting in-school suspension. Although, on my first Friday (I had arrived at the Academy on a Sunday night), I had a delivery. Sonic called me on the intercom to come to the front of the school. He gave me a parcel wrapped in brown paper tied up with a small white string. I went back to my dorm. Neon was sparring with Leon, Omalic was making up a test in Allitode's room, and Yosh was in the hospital wing for taking a nasty tumble with an arrow after going backward over a rock. Rocks seemed to be pretty dangerous and common here.

Since I was in the room alone, I checked the package. It read: *To: Motorthud From: Forest Girl and Bunny*. It looked like I had received a gift from Shiro and Furry! I eagerly unwrapped it and found a book. It had no words inside, no title, cover, or even page numbers. I had a journal.

I started thinking that it wasn't that bad. After all, a present's a present. And I was feeling a bit homesick since I had no idea where my real home was, or if I even had one. I grabbed a pen off the table and wrote my name to see what the pages were like. It stayed on the page for three seconds, then disappeared. I checked the pen. It wasn't an invisible ink pen, but when I wrote in the book again, words still disappeared.

I was annoyed, so I wrote, *Hey! Will you stop messing around, you darn book!*

The words disappeared again, but a new line of text came up saying, *Dude, chill out. It's just us. LOL.*

I jumped back in surprise. Well, now I knew I could contact them if I needed to. But I had classes and I was already late for lunch. I put the book in my backpack and hurried to the top floor, after writing *Gtg, bbl.*

The weather was light and breezy, so we all sat nearest the edges of the cafeteria. After I picked up my lunch, Major tripped me AND I had to share my meal with Omalic. It didn't make me furious but it did aggravate me a bit.

Later in archery, however, when I was getting my arrows from the target, Major fired more at the target that I was collecting them from and I had to dodge several of his scarily precise shots.

After Major ran out of arrows, Kardon, the teacher, said to me, "This is an archery range, not a playground. I expect you to stay after class and clean this target."

I heard Major slightly laughing. "Yes, sir," I grumbled. But what really ticked me off happened in secrecy class.

When Loi, the teacher, tried on certain disguises, Major, in the seat next to me, crowed, "That thing looks like you threw a rat on your face!" When Loi turned around, Major pointed at me which gave me *another* time to stay after class.

At the end of the day, I was pretty fed up with Major and Sonic noticed it after I was swimming. "Hello, Motor! What seems to be the matter?"

I looked near the hospital. Sonic was leaving, just turning the key to lock up.

"It's just that Major has been annoying me all day. It's nothing."

"It doesn't look like nothing. You look like you could use some relaxation. Try taking a walk in the forest." He pointed to the left of the hospital to the insanely huge gathering of trees. There were even trees growing on top of trees! "It's how I relieve my stress after a long, hard day of work." This was the first time one of Sonic's ideas made sense.

"That's a pretty good idea, Sonic. See you later."

"Okay, but don't stay in too long! There are spooky stories of ghosts living there. Ooooooo!" And then Sonic was back to his usual, crazy self.

Sonic was right, though, and the chittering of the late afternoon birds made my mind wander freely and joyfully. I hummed to the sounds of nature and ended up wandering around. At one point, when I had my eyes closed, I breathed in the light forest scent. I stumbled flat on my face over a rock (I swear, they're out to get me). "Stupid nature," I mumbled, as I got back up. I looked down, but the rock wasn't natural—it was man-made. And had some sort of carvings on it. *Whiteisa 1398-1467. Slain for fear of Slenderman.*

Who is this Whiteisa? I thought, *and what was so bad about a Slender-whatsit that they needed to kill someone?* I squinted to read the text, and now noticed it was well past darkness outside. I went to leave but saw another gravestone. *Edhe 1996-2014. Unknown slaying motive.* This was getting creepy. The place obviously wasn't a graveyard, based on how old yet legible the writing was, but now, looking back on what Sonic said about ghosts, I was extremely nervous.

I looked around quickly to find a way out, but the darkness took the form of trees. I shook, panted, and felt like I was about to need a new pair of pants if so much as a squirrel came out of a shrub. I heard my heart pounding in my ears, my head swiftly searching from side to side for a sign of a way out, of just any clear path to safety. That was when I came to a halt and saw *it*.

It wasn't the way out. I couldn't have had worse luck. *It* was a creature that could easily touch the treetops. *It* was a creature with few facial features. *It* was a creature with its eyes full of hatred, denial, and solitude. *It* had long, black fingers, with black tentacles sprouting out of its back. *It* was no ordinary creature. *It* was a monster to slay all monsters. The Slenderman.

I stifled back a scream and leapt backward onto the grave as its dark tentacles reached out toward me. I inched over the grave as the ominous hands reached to me farther and farther. When I was behind the gravestone, the monster looked quite fearful. I backed up more to see if it was trying to distract me and my hand brushed against the back of the stone. It lit up with a brilliant blue light, and a shadow came blasting out of the ground in front of me. It screamed, and the sound was full of rejection and despair. I nearly fainted. The Slenderman looked at the shadow in fear, and when the shadow raised a hand to the monster, the Slenderman disappeared. The shadow then turned to me, looking like a king.

"Who dares awaken the Lord Whiteisa?" the shadow said in an ancient and powerful, royal voice. The figure had a long black cape that whooshed when he turned. He wore dark armor all over, but his eyes were full of something that I couldn't place—full of red. I was so startled by what just happened, all I could do was murmur, "Merp—mer, meep!"

"Well, this surely can't be the hero to awaken me! Too frail and weak!" he exclaimed. I was greatly offended.

"I am not weak! Now, what in the name of Arch just happened?"

He seemed to smile. "Well, I must say. Courageous, bold, and a bit loud-mouthed. Certainly the hero."

"Well, I don't have any clue what you're talking about," I said, trying to respect Furry's wishes. "Now, who, or what, are you?" He pointed to the side of the grave my hand brushed against. I saw a strange tale embedded on the back.

"Within the edge of the Vaalbara, there was a king, Whiteisa. Clad in black he lived in his rich kingdom. He was a ruler of that edge of the Vaalbara where he lived in pleasure and subsistence. With him at his side was his loyal pet, his Slenderman. It was the king's dream to build his frontier, a castle where none could challenge him. Yet, they did challenge and affront him. Those of that realm had the gallows ready for him, as his 'pet' had been plaguing the towns and fighting off the loved ones of the king's enemies. He perished, yet killed from the beyond, for his Slenderman had slain all who came across his path, grieving over his master. So the ruler became a ghost plagued to continue to do his goal as it was in life, and in death—to build his castle with his Slenderman, who still haunts this land, but only obeys his dead master, even to this day."

I looked back up at the shadow, er, Whiteisa. He was still staring down at me. "You ordered the monster to do that?" He sounded like a tyrant worthy of nobody's respect or time if he did horrible things like killing people.

"Oh, Nether, no! I merely whispered to my subjects that my enemies should all be killed off as a joke. But heavens, creatures can change things around in their heads quite easily."

That made him seem a bit more innocent to me. "So who were your enemies?" If I was talking to a ghost, I might as well get some information out of him.

"They were, as you now call them, 'The Dark Ones.' Nasty, you think so?"

"Were you one of them?"

He seemed taken aback. "I beg your pardon! I may be a ghost, but no stereotyping, sir! If I was one of them, I would have been reincarnated decades ago! But I will always lend a helping hand to you people, the . . ." He squinted to look at the crest that was on my sword hilt. "Knights of Archlinder. I don't know what it is, but the name is familiar. That was our neighboring realm, I believe. Ah yes, we traded and came over often and became great allies."

"You would help us?" It sounded too good to be true.

"Why of course!" A thought then crossed my mind.

"Wait. You're a ghost. Can you do anything?" He seemed insulted by the question. I knew I had chosen the wrong thing to say.

"Anything? I'll show you *anything*!" He turned into a mist and swirled into my body. It felt like ice going down my back, but I couldn't stop it. I felt him take control of my body. He then made me punch myself in the face over and over again. I could only feel and hear him say, "Stop hitting yourself! Stop hitting yourself!" Eventually, he gave up and left, leaving me out of breath and hurt.

"Okay, that was pretty cool. And . . . ow!"

"Sorry, a bit too rough on the hero? Does he want some warm milk and a blankee before he gets tucked in?"

"Dude . . ." I mumbled angrily, hand reaching for sword.

"Calm down! I don't need another death on my hands! I will help you all through thick and thin! And I'll be sure to tell my pet, too." I sighed with relief when he said that last part. His "pet" really gave me the willies.

"You'd better leave. People will be wondering what happened." It seems pretty late out.

He had a good point. "But how can I do that? I don't remember how I even ended up in here!"

"You mind letting me take you over again?"

I applied a forceful look.

"What? I'm only going to lead you back! You won't even remember it! I swear on my mortal body!"

"Fine," I said, "But be sure to—"

But he had already swirled into my body like a mist, and all I saw was black.

Chapter 10
THE GAME OF DEATH

"M otor? Motor? Hello?" I threw my pillow tiredly at the person shouting into my ear. My eyes opened to see Omalic standing over my bed.

"What time is it?" I moaned.

"It's eight o' clock. Why are you so tired?" he asked, examining my crusty eyes.

"Because I . . ." I couldn't explain Whiteisa to anyone. He promised me when I was being taken over that if I told, he would take over a Dark One's body, find my dorm, and . . . well, you know the rest.

"Because I . . . got lost in the forest late last night." It *was* the truth.

"Well, you are gonna be so pumped up for this!" said Omalic. "We got tickets to the Stewieville Spleef Tournaments!"

The Stewieville Spleef Tournaments? I was wide awake in a second. Those things were sold out for months! Yosh and I usually discussed the teams we bet on, but we never thought of actually being able to go there.

"How did you get them?" I asked enthusiastically.

Omalic replied with joy. "Easy! Buzzy invited us to the game! Says he has a part-time job there or something. Cool, right?"

"The best!" I said, full of energy. "But what about the others?"

"Oh, right. Well, he already invited you, Neon, Yosh, and me. Neon and Yosh arrived ahead of time to meet the players. The game starts soon. Come on!"

I leapt out of bed to the door, took a quick shower, and dashed with Omalic out the Academy door. "How are we going to get there?" I asked. I never really thought about transportation much.

"I borrowed my dad's ship. It's a bit old, but she'll pull through."

It didn't really look as if there was a way to the arena by water since the attraction was in the desert. I gave him a doubtful look.

"No, not that kind of ship." Omalic pressed a button on a keychain, and I heard a honk above us. I looked up to see a bright red, streamlined jet that hovered about ten feet above us. A ladder rolled out one side of the ship's doors, and we climbed inside.

There was a pilot's dashboard, wide window view, and enough room for about four people. The floor was a smear-proof glass, so you could see out below. It also had air conditioning, electricity, and a mini-fridge. Everything was eco-friendly, since it was powered by corn syrup.

Omalic's voice came on the intercom overhead. "This is your captain speaking, and we are headed to the Stewieville Spleef Arena, which is about fifteen minutes away. Please fasten your seat belts and enjoy your flight."

I had never been in any sort of jet before to my knowledge, so the floating feeling was unnatural. It was weird after only knowing about traveling on foot, being controlled by gravity. The flight was scary at first; going upward so much it felt like the ship was about to explode. But after that, the ride felt nice and natural. In exactly fifteen minutes, just like Omalic said, we reached several dozen ships floating in front of us.

"Parking lot," Omalic explained. He let the ladder drop down, and we climbed down to the Stewieville Spleef Arena, a black stadium with enough room for hundreds of spectators in the stands, an announcer's booth, an overhead glass dome, and the main arena, full of the usual regulation snow cubes.

I guess I should explain what spleefing really is. In spleef, there is no gravity to make the snow blocks fall, but players stay on the ground or jump over it. There is a small layer between the players and the lava waiting for them below, which was usually the gravity-defying, climate-controlled snow. The two players dug holes with their shovels, quickly, around one another, and whoever accidentally fell in the lava lost. There are usually branching tournaments, where each team fights for power. In the end, it's a game of death—looks like the matador kind of entertainment might be coming back into style.

We walked in the entryway, which was small and dingy compared to . . . well, anything. But the arena was enormous. It had a pit, seats around the pit, and a glass dome. The field looked red, and I was sure that it wasn't lava. We found Neon and Yosh in the front row. Buzzy must've had a vital job there, judging by the great seats he had gotten us.

I looked at the cleaning crew, but Buzzy wasn't there. I checked the vendors, but he wasn't handing out peanuts and knickknacks. Then I heard a familiar voice echo around the stadium.

"Ladies and gentlemen, what a wonder of work that was for Stewie, not just a master spleefer, but also the owner of this arena."

I saw a man in a blue-and-black jumpsuit with a creeper face on it (the Chicago Creeper uniform) hop out of the pit.

"Give him a hand folks, give him a hand!" I looked up to the announcer's box to see Buzzy mouth to me, *Like the seats?* He then flashed me a thumbs-up, and I returned it. Being an announcer is a "difficult" job, so that explained the great privileges and bonuses.

"What's the score anyway?" I asked Yosh.

"Chicago Creepers are beating the Zambeque Zombies, three to one. Also, I got this free yo-yo signed by Stewie!"

He held up a black and blue yo-yo with Stewie's signature sprawled across it. I returned my focus to the game. Next up it was Zero, another Chicago creeper, versus someone named Hosoidallas. They each started out in their corners, glaring menacingly at each other.

Once Buzzy yelled, "Go!", the two jumped forward at each other like jungle cats over an antelope and dug around one another. At one point, Hoso was running backward from Zero and didn't notice the empty space behind him. It was gruesome, the way lava melts people. The crowd cheered at Zero's victory, and now it was four to one. This was gonna be a piece of cake.

The score eventually turned to the Zambeque Zombies and was tied at four to four. It was also time for a break, so I went outside to get some fresh air. Even though it was a desert, it was still nice. I was just going forward to get a drink from a cactus—

"There you are! C'mon, get in and get into uniform!" A hand forcefully "escorted" me back inside to the athlete's entrance. I had no idea what was going on, but the guy sounded pretty big, so I decided not to argue with him. He dragged me into the blue door, the one leading to the Creepers' suiting room. He put the blue-and-black jumpsuit over me, and I knew where it was probably going from there.

Whoever had grabbed me at the entrance must have thought I was an athlete and gotten me ready for the next fight. *Although*, I wondered, *how could they have thought I was an athlete? I would've already been wearing the uniform.* I didn't have time to think because they forcefully thrust a shovel into my hands and pushed me into the arena, closing the team door behind me. I was dead.

Apparently, I was the tie-breaker, so *of course* I had to go up against the beefiest guy on the other team! He was shirtless, had a long yellow beard, a leather and steel helmet, and he clutched his shovel like a murder weapon in one hand, his bulging muscles rippling with power. But with my good fortune, the pain below would only last a few seconds. When I came out, everyone in the crowd cheered. Why didn't they recognize me? Why didn't they pull me out of here? Then I realized they had put a bandana, to match the jumpsuit, right over my face. That explained it.

I looked up to the crowd for reassurance. There wasn't much; Neon, Omalic, and Yosh were trading athlete cards, and Buzzy was announcing an ad for hot dogs. But all at once, the crowd started yelling, "Three, two, one, fight!"

The opponent ran forward, but I stood in my area, shaking. When he was only a meter away, I hit the small area with my shovel, and it collapsed into the lava. He quickly sidestepped and started chasing after me again. I dragged my shovel along my side, causing the line of the snow to fall. At one point, I leaned a little too far to the right and nearly plummeted face first into the burning liquid, but I used the shovel to push myself back up from a nearby pile of snow.

Eventually, I had to jump around because of the major holes everywhere. At that point though, I guess the Zambeque Zombie couldn't take it any longer, and he started swinging at me with his shovel.

Then I had an idea. *If he can't play by the rules, then I won't either.* I stopped in front of him and dropped to my knees. I heard someone shout, "What's he doing?"

Wait for it, I thought. The opponent rushed up with a smile on his face and shifted his shovel to behind his back. *Wait for it.* He picked up the shovel and swung it forward. *Now!* I simply leapt to the side, avoiding the strike. He looked off balance and that's when I rushed behind him and pushed him. Into the hole in the snow. Into lava. Into his death.

I quickly looked away, but after a tense moment of silence, the crowd cheered. Everyone rushed into the arena, shouting, "The Creepers won! The Creepers won!"

I rushed over to my friends before anyone could lift me on their shoulders. Omalic instantly sprinted up to me once I was at their row. He was so excited, he said what sounded like, "OhmygoshthatwastotallyamazingcanIhaveyourautograph-nonevermindIdon'twanttowasteyourtime" but I stopped him short when I pulled off the jumpsuit and bandana.

Neon recovered first. "Motor? That was *you*? What happened?"

"I don't know, but I don't think it was an accident."

◆　　◆　　◆

Afterward, we were back in the hovercraft to the Academy. Omalic was checking out the jumpsuit I used, too obsessed with the team and its memorabilia to notice I had almost died. We also received a bunch of stuff from Stewie as an apology for the situation. It didn't really cover for it though, as you can't erase an image from your mind like death. Buzzy was flying us back to the Academy, while Neon and Yosh asked how I got into this mess and how I thought it happened.

"For the eighth time, I don't know." But they just wouldn't let up.

"Come on, you have to Motor!" Yosh complained. "At least tell us who you think it might be."

Then, I had a strange vision. I imagined the spleef arena, filled to the brim with fans from everywhere. Then, I saw one face stand out from the rest in the crowd. His face was hidden by the bandana, but the blue-and-black jumpsuit didn't lie. I snapped back to reality.

"Now, I might have a slight idea," I said, baring my teeth in anger and frustration.

Chapter II
GOING UNDERCOVER

I REALIZED THAT TO FIND WHO SET ME UP FOR THIS SPLEEF MATCH, I had to get to them in secret. So on Monday, I paid as much attention as I could in Secrecy, taught by Loiwol.

"Now, if I chose to hide out in a public area, what kind of costume would I wear?" he asked.

Geo raised his hand and replied, "It depends on the area."

Loiwol went over and rubbed Geo's head. "Yes, that's it, my faithful little prodigy. If you're wearing cold clothes, like a parka, in Scorpion Gulch, that *might* get you noticed. You've got to dress like the locals! But also, be sure to dress to hide yourself from anyone noticing you. If you're going to Scorpion Gulch, wear light clothing or a veil! And if you're in a city up north like New Kobol, wear an overcoat! The overcoat will easily hide the face, and so will the veil."

He noted to blend into the crowd. After saying to stay out of dark alleys, he dismissed the class. Everyone filed out of the room, happy after a long day to practice swords and relax. I stayed behind and walked up to Loiwol's desk, where he looked up at me.

"Oh, hello Motor! I saw you writing down lots of notes today! Very nice! What is up?"

"I wanted to know what your first secret mission was."

He sat down, putting his hands together with an uneasy look on his face. "Oh. Okay, then." He sighed. "It was 2163. I was invading the—"

"Actually sir, that's not what I meant," I interrupted. "I just want to know how you stayed 'under the radar.' You know?"

He suddenly looked happier. "Oh, why didn't you just say so? I always moved silently when following, tried to follow where the crowd was going and what they were doing, and I never told *anyone* what I was doing."

Everything seemed a lot easier now. "Thanks, sir," I told him as I dashed out of the classroom. I ran all the way from Loiwol's class to the dorm, locking the door behind me. I instantly got a sheet of paper from my backpack and a pen, too. I figured that the person who had sabotaged me would come to the spleef arena again, so I noted to ask Buzzy for tickets again. Then, I created scenes of how I should follow the enemy. There was a lot of erasing, as many scenarios had flaws where I could be caught. At last, after working nearly four hours, I had finally come up with the plan.

Just as I was putting it away, Neon and Omalic walked in, covered in sweat. I nervously shoved the plan in my backpack so fast I fell over onto the floor. They just looked at me and started laughing. "Not funny, guys," I said.

They took a few seconds to stop, then Neon finally said, "Sorry, Motor. Just got back from the cage match, and there wasn't much humor in there. What were you doing?"

I opened my mouth to tell them, but then I remembered what Loiwol had said: *Never tell anyone what you're doing.*

"Uh, it was just a lot of homework," I said.

"Oh, cool. We should probably start on ours. Kardon's got us working on a homework mountain," Omalic huffed.

Not long after Omalic and Neon started archery homework, Yosh showed up, explaining that his uncle took him to a movie and that's why he was late. An hour after Yosh arrived and we were playing "Spleef, the Board Game," it was lights out. I was climbing into bed when I realized that I had to protect my plan in case it landed in the wrong hands. When the lights were out, I stealthily slid the plan under the bed, then taped it to the top of the bed's underside. I knew I could rest safe now. There wasn't a chance of my plan slipping into the wrong hands.

◆   ◆   ◆

The days rolled slowly past, but at last, it was Saturday. I had been acting a little suspicious around my dorm mates because on Friday, Neon asked what was going on.

I nervously replied, "What? Nothing's wrong! I'm just my regular old self!" I soon learned it wasn't the best thing to say, after I read a book from the library where some guy says the same thing and is found decapitated in a river.

I had woken up early on that Saturday morning to go meet Buzzy by the Academy pool. Buzzy pressed a button on his key-chain, and I saw the enormous hovercraft. It was blue and black and had the blue familiar face on the sides of it. It was obvious Buzzy was a fan of the Chicago Creepers. It was the same style of the jet Omalic and I had ridden in, but the inside wasn't that different either. It had the same floor and seats and the same captain's chair, but this one had an LCD TV, a regular kitchen, and a massage chair. I looked at Buzzy with my jaw dropped.

"All the benefits of being an announcer," he said, and left me standing in the main area.

In about ten minutes, we reached the arena. I scurried down the ladder just in time to get my seat and watch the game. I tried to look interested, but I was really scanning the crowd. At last, I saw him. The blue-and-black jumpsuit hid in the crowd like a pebble on a beach, but I found him. I kept my eye on him the whole time, but not directly at him because he would be wondering, *Why the heck is this creep staring at me?* So, as Loiwol would do, I tried to stay under the radar.

A couple of players got a really good score, but I didn't pay much attention. But then, my target strolled into the pit. Then I discovered this wasn't part of my "perfect" plan. I needed him to stay alive, so I could know what he was up to. If he died, I might be in huge danger.

But then again, this arena had some help for me, at least. After running through it about four times, I finally had all I needed to help me get info out of this guy, while keeping him alive: three rolls of toilet paper, a bag of peanuts, and a basket of hot nachos with Blaze sauce. Since I was in the front row, it would be a lot easier to finish the plan. As soon as the round started, my near-assassin was about to get hit by the opponent's shovel, when I tossed the nachos. When it hit the enemy's face, I could already see his skin turning red. He started running around like a maniac until he slipped into a hole in the pit and met something even hotter: the lava.

The rest of the rounds went on in this fashion. When the enemy was running at my assassin, I threw the toilet paper, causing them to slip and fall, sometimes face-first in the deep end of the boiling contents below. The nachos were for when the enemy was close to hitting my main man. The peanuts?

Well, even Knights of Archlinder get hungry sometimes. By the end, my assassin's team had won, he was actually alive, and everyone left the stadium. I left with the crowd, but slowly kept my eye on the assassin.

By the time I got outside, he went back into the athlete's entrance. This was it. Being specific down to this very moment, I pulled on the jumpsuit Stewie had lent me as an apology for being forced to fight for my life. I wandered into the blue room, and the lights shut off. I figured out at that moment that I *might* have been a *bit* obvious with the "random" objects flying into the pit. All I remembered next was some footsteps, a couple of blows to my head, and I blacked out.

◆　◆　◆

"So, what do we have here? Hey boys, this is the best the Knights can do? Just throw in an ugly rookie? Ha! They never were the strongest sword in the chest, were they?"

I strained to look at three figures staring above me and heard the laughter that followed my captor's mocking. I was in a chair with my arms tied behind my back and a piece of tape over my mouth. Really original.

I instantly recognized one of the figures as the yellow-bearded, muscle-bulging, monster of an opponent that I had faced last week. The grimace was still on his face, but he shouldn't have been here or even alive! The last time I had seen him, I saw a burning mass of dying life. What had happened? I couldn't recognize the person to my captor's left. However, he was tall, had a quiver of arrows in a small bag, and menacing scars on his face that said, *Hi, I'm your worst nightmare! And who might you be?*

The only person that really stood out was the one in the middle. The blue-and-black jumpsuit, the bandana, the stoic and heroic-looking face. My captor. The one I thought I could trust. My new worst enemy. Stewie.

"Well, let's see who this little sneak really is," he said. He tore off my bandana and looked stunned for a second, but quickly recovered. "Well, I should've known the person spying on me would be the one I shoved into my game. Right, fellas?" The two nodded in agreement, and he returned to directly talk to me. "You think your whole 'legend thing' is secret, don't ya? Ha! I've spied harder listening to karaoke tapes! Okay, so it doesn't make sense . . . but, well, ya know what I mean! I was in Ida's Castle spyin' on y'all! I heard every word! You think you can rise up and defeat me? I've killed mice bigger than you!"

My eyes widened at the mention of Ida's Castle.

"That so precious to ya, huh? Edhe! Go unwrap his mouth so we can hear him cry his guts out!"

The name sounded familiar. Edhe. Then I remembered back to Whiteisa. What was the name on the grave next to his? It was Edhe! Wait . . . he had a grave before I got to that forest, died when I beat him at spleef, and now he's ripping the tape off my mouth. I'm pretty sure it wasn't a coincidence. He had the same muscles, same long, yellow beard, but he had died twice, possibly even more! It couldn't have been the same one. Could it?

After near howling in pain when the tape was ripped off, I asked, "Okay, you are a spleef arena owner and a multi-millionaire. Who are you, really?"

His already wide grin turned into an evil, creepy, wicked smile. I didn't like where this was going.

"Who am I? Let's see . . . I've been spying on ya, waiting for ya, setting ya up. Who *do* you think I am?"

I thought Sonicar at first, but then I realized Stewie's not the crazy-doctor type. But the real answer was evident. I remembered what everyone had been calling *them*. Stewie got a glint in his eyes.

"Yep. I'm one of them. A Dark One."

I would've gasped if we were on reality television, but we weren't, so I just tried to look as if I had known it all along.

"Oh, you didn't know it all along, Motorthud. I, er, we," he gestured to the two others around him, "are Dark Ones. Boys, change position."

I braced for them to change into a running stance and cut me in half, but they didn't. They lifted their sleeves and I saw a tattoo of . . . well, the figure kept changing like a figure in the reflection of a murky puddle of water. When Edhe touched his, he disappeared. Or, that's what it seemed like. In his place was a seven-foot long anaconda with yellow, slitted eyes and poison-tipped fangs. It seemed hungry for prey, or me. The other man, the one with the many scars, touched his and transformed into an eight-foot-tall boar with red, steely eyes, razor-sharp tusks, and death on its breath.

Stewie transformed into the worst of all. He touched his tattoo and turned into a dark purple figure with midnight black robes, dark red eyes under his shawl, and a purple ax with a few bloodstains on the end. He was prepared for victory over death.

He uttered two words that froze my blood.

"Kill. Now."

As the two creatures lunged forward, I closed my eyes and braced for death. But it never came. Instead, a hiss emanated, and the wall behind the two creatures exploded. In the remains of the wall stood three figures I knew quite well. "Yosh, Neon,

Omalic! Help!" They probably knew that before they even came in because once the wall was down, the battle had begun.

Neon took his silver ax and sliced the ropes binding me to the chair apart. Meanwhile, Yosh faced the snake with his trusted silver sword, while Omalic faced the giant boar with the creature's leftover arrows and bow. As soon as I was freed, Neon and I turned toward Stewie, just as his moonlight ax danced across the room, right over our heads, and flew sailing back into his hand.

We both rushed toward him, but before we could attack him, he instantly teleported to the other side of the room, almost getting me beheaded by Neon's ax. I then thought we could each go to one side of the room. He seemed to understand.

Omalic was still facing the boar, as Yosh was with the snake, neither with any luck. After Neon and I separated to our sides of the room, Stewie teleported to mine. I retreated to the middle just as Stewie tried to slice through my back. I gestured for Neon to come in the middle, too, and he followed. Stewie looked happy about this, thinking we surrendered. He had kept trying to kill me off, but now it was a two-in-one knight package.

He spun his midnight ax around, and it launched toward us quickly. I held my sword out in front of me, waiting for the ax to come. Just as the ax was about to kill off Neon and I, I shifted my sword so it was right into Stewie's ax's wooden tip at the end and spun it around through the air. It was now swinging right toward our would-be undertaker.

I saw something in Stewie's eyes. Surprise? Fear? But he would deserve this. The weapon flew to and got caught in Stewie's chest, launching him across the room. Neon and I rushed over to the dark figure and saw that he was fading, like when a TV signal goes out.

"Motor. You got . . . the best of me with your . . . two-shoes partners. I will now leave this body, thanks to you, kind soul."

I thought he was a demon who took over the real Stewie's body, so I started to let him go and turned around. But then, as I was walking away from him, I heard a strange, metallic buzz. I faced the dark figure again, only this time, he was smirking.

I called to Neon, Yosh, and Omalic. They all turned in the direction I was facing and saw the horrible enemy we all had to face. Stewie had jumped onto the boar, both perfectly fine, and he also grabbed the snake, still hungry, and swung it around, ready to use it as a poisonous living whip. Now we all had to face a giant boar with a nearly unstoppable demon riding it, armed with a snake as a whip. Great. Just perfect.

I motioned to the others that we had to change our strategies. They all nodded in agreement. We yelled "For Archlinder!" and the final battle began. Neon, Yosh, and I faced the boar on the ground while Omalic battled Stewie's snake whip. I observed the boar for its weakness when I noticed the tusks. They were razor-sharp, but—

"Yosh! Neon!" I yelled. "Try to slash at the tusks!"

The boar, unfortunately, also heard me, and started sweeping the two aside with his steel walls. He shook his head to get them out of the way but was so distracted that he didn't even see Yosh holding his sword out in front of him to the side of the boar's head. The creature squealed in pain and was paralyzed for half a minute. I climbed on top of the head, just as I saw Omalic coming up from the other side. We both faced Stewie as Omalic drew out his bow. I doubted Stewie could be defeated with just a bow, but I realized Omalic had a different idea.

He held it back so far that the arrow glowed with a red light. Stewie then shifted the snake to Omalic in hopes of killing him, but that's what Omalic was waiting for. He launched the flaming arrow into the snake's mouth as it struck out for him, going through the snake, lighting him on fire, out the snake's end, and stopped going just as Omalic caught it below. I now saw how skilled Omalic was with creative weapons.

The boar regained control and shook Omalic and I off his head. Stewie threw the now-dead snake aside and readied for our attacks. Stewie kicked the boar in the flanks, and the boar let out a squeal so loud, we all actually *flew* across the room. It then charged to the corner in which I had landed. I was about to become roadkill, but at that moment, a chair flung by Yosh made an arc through the air and hit the boar right in the eye. The boar became so angry, I thought it was about to breathe fire.

It blasted, full speed, toward Yosh, opening its mouth to scream, when Yosh stepped aside to reveal Omalic, who instantly launched the arrow into the boar's wide-open mouth. As it hit the back of the boar's throat, smoke started pouring from the animal's ears, and it collapsed in a heap on the floor. I later realized that the arrow Omalic used to kill the snake was launched into the boar. It was still on fire, but also, since it had traveled through the snake's mouth, it was coated in poison.

As soon as the boar fell over, Stewie was pinned underneath it. We surrounded him, our weapons readied.

"Well," panted Stewie, "it looks like you knights killed my minions—again. The Empire will not be very happy. But fortunately, I have tons of allies to chip away at the lands of Vaalbara until it is all ours. But be warned: the darkness is spreading." He started to fade, becoming less visible by the second.

"Wait!" I yelled. He looked toward me. "Are you the one in command?"

A wide grin appeared on his face. "No, Motor, there are more of us. Many of us. Some even stronger than me. And we are all after one thing. You." He disappeared after those words in a collection of purple smoke and black fire. But he wasn't dead. He had probably already spread word of the battle, and more assassins might have been after me right now.

"So," Omalic said after the long silence when Stewie left, "what was all that about? Them trying to kill you and all that?"

I sighed. Now that they had been in a battle because of me and saved my butt, I couldn't lie anymore. I dragged them into this mess; they deserved to hear it.

"Okay," I said, "I'll tell you. But don't tell anyone. Archlinder Swear?"

We all put our hands in a circle and swore to the god. I started by telling of how I woke up with no memory, all the way up until the present.

"Oh my Arch!" Yosh said. "That's just insane! *You're* the hero to save Vaal? Have mercy on me!" He bowed down and started kissing the ground in front of me.

"Easy, Yosh," I said. "Just, don't. It's fine."

"Right," he said. "No praising. Just keep it cool."

We all boarded Omalic's hovercraft after that and started flying toward the Academy under a bright blue, cloudless sky. I hoped that was what my future was going to be like. Clear skies all the way.

Chapter 12
THE EMPIRE

FTER STEWIE WAS DEFEATED, I WONDERED ABOUT THE "empire" he had talked about. *"The Empire will not be very happy."* And what worse could they have than Stewie? He did say that there were some stronger than him. I hoped that number was small. After I got back to the Academy from the battle, I ran for the desk on which the book Shiro and Furry had sent me sat. I opened it hastily, grabbed a pen, and started writing.

"Just defeated some Dark Ones. Stewie is a Dark One! He and lackeys had strange transforming tattoos. Please write back ASAP." It didn't take long for a comment to appear after my words had faded away.

"Will investigate and be on lookout. Told Ida and she said to be suspicious of Dark Ones nearby! Also, she may send help. Shiro out fishing right now. Signed, Furry."

I felt a sense of dread when I looked over the part about Ida's help. She was a good friend, but after seeing her and her castle, I wasn't so sure that the help would work. A wolf to help me would be cool, but it was too risky since the Academy had a strict "no-pets" policy. There couldn't be any people, either, because the Academy's dorms were already full and had no more space left for another knight. At least I had Neon, who was still help from Ida—sort of. But until the help arrived, I would be on the lookout, just like Furry said to.

But the question of this "Empire" was still running through my mind endlessly. I asked Omalic to see what he thought about what it might mean, but he gave me a strange look. "It's pretty weird, but I don't think Stewie and other Dark Ones would be playing baseball," Omalic responded.

I replied, "No, Stewie's *empire*, not *umpire*!"

Omalic opened his mouth to speak, but I quickly replied, "And no, he does not have a legion of *vampires*. I just want to know what, or where, you think Stewie's empire might be."

"I dunno," he said, "but I'm totally looking forward to the field trip to New Kobol City!"

With the battle with Stewie and some tests still going through my mind, I forgot all about the trip. The Academy was going on a field trip to New Kobol City, the most populous city in Vaal. It had a lot of shops, entertainment, great restaurants and fantastic plays at Pangea Theater. However, only the students who hadn't had detention in the last week could go, meaning Major and Cooster couldn't go because of Tuesday's incident where there was tear gas in Acy's hot dog.

New Kobol City sounded nice. Major wouldn't be there, and the Dark Ones couldn't be anywhere close by. It was perfect. Because of the "can't get detention to go" detail, I made sure to stay out of trouble by just doing the usual schoolwork and messaging Furry and Shiro every once in a while. And it worked!

Eventually, Friday arrived. I packed my backpack with my camera, a water bottle, my wallet, and some pretzels in case I needed a snack. I put on my "Kobol Kings" (New Kobol's spleef team) pin and examined myself in the mirror. I was ready for the day with a smile that said "I can't lose today!", but not a smile that said, "Help! Get this grin off my face; it's killing me!"

Neon rushed in the room. "Motor, come on! The jet's gonna leave soon! Don't wanna miss your first visit to New Kobol!"

I shoved my stuff into my backpack, and Neon and I sprinted out of the Academy, up the ladder, and into the school jet.

It wasn't as nice as Omalic and Buzzy's jets. It was a regular school one with some windows, a stern-faced pilot, and hard leather seats. Despite the appearance of the school jet, I was still ecstatic to be able to go to New Kobol. But for some reason, I was worried. I don't know why, because I was going to one of the greatest cities in Vaal, and should be excited. But still, the feeling stayed, like glue on paper.

After I passed flight time by playing a spleef card game with Yosh, the jet finally slowed down to a halt on top of a low-rise brick building that looked like it had been condemned years ago. Omalic, Yosh, Neon, and I all jumped out of our seats to be the first ones out into the grand city.

We all toppled out onto the pavement and set off as a group, seeing a welcome sign first. "Welcome to New Kobol City! Home of the Kobol Kings! Enjoy your stay!" Then we all walked down the sidewalk.

"What do you guys wanna see first?" Yosh asked.

My stomach rumbled.

"How about we grab some breakfast first? I know a great place down the street," Neon said.

He led us to a restaurant that had bacon-flavored bagels and omelets coated in brown sugar. It sounded gross, but anything with bacon was worth a try for me.

"Is bacon perfect in everything?" Omalic asked when we entered the restaurant. Neon took a sample and told him, "If you don't believe it, try it." He shoved the food into Omalic's mouth.

Omalic started to protest, but his eyes lit up at once. "My Arch, this is the best food I've ever tasted!" he exclaimed, and once he said that, we were all eager to start eating.

After the delicious breakfast, we went to Pangea Theater to see some play about a guy who's a monster but still finds love. Kinda awkward with all us guys in there while the rest of the crowd were mainly women. We left early after the part where all the girls in the theater go, "Aww! So cute!"

We had no idea what they meant by that. We mainly went shopping for stuff after that, and I even found a spleef video game! Although, because of Stewie, I didn't think I'd play as the Chicago Creepers.

A while later, we all split up to see different things, so we decided to meet back in the main square in half an hour. I couldn't think of anywhere to go, so I rambled along the streets, checking out some stores that looked interesting. But while I was walking, the heavy feeling in my stomach from earlier came down harder than ever before. I knew the breakfast I had was insanely huge, but that didn't cause the feeling. I tried to walk it off. The feeling wouldn't leave. I thought I should see Sonic about it for some medicine, but when I turned around, I saw it—a large, square, black and gold tower, with a lot more black than any other color. It nearly reached the clouds and had a pinnacle at the top that looked menacing. Almost as if it could harness the lightning, it got up there and used it on me. Just add some dark storm clouds and vultures to the building, and it would have looked exactly like haunted houses in the movies. At that very moment, the feeling in my stomach dropped even lower. I felt like I was going to puke. I sprinted full speed toward the main square, not even checking to see if it was time for all of us to meet. Luckily, I saw Neon sitting near a fountain, eating a ham sandwich.

"Neon!" I exclaimed as I dashed to him. Right before I was about to crash head-first into him, my heels skidded to a halt on the ground.

"Motor, what the heck's going on? Mugger after you?" he asked.

I was out of breath running, so most words couldn't escape my mouth. "Huge tower . . . Dark Ones . . . gut feeling . . . oh my Arch," I managed to wheeze out.

"Uh, sorry," he said. "Don't speak exhausted. Have a sip of water and try again."

I snatched the water bottle and drank until I could breathe normally again.

"You know how Stewie said something about an empire when we defeated him?"

Neon nodded. "Yeah. So?"

"So, that's all I could concentrate on in the past week! Then, I had a bad feeling in my gut when we were heading here. And when I was walking around, the feeling got worse when I saw this huge skyscraper. I have a feeling in my gut that the Dark Ones are there."

"Are you sure you're all right?" he asked. "Sonic's back on the ship. If you're sick or something—"

"Dude, I'm not crazy!" I cut in. "I can show you the tower right now! But I have a bad feeling if we don't do something soon, something terrible will happen to New Kobol!"

"Okay then, okay," Neon said. "I can text Omalic and Yosh now to meet us here since we're all in on this business against the Dark Ones together."

Neon whipped out a red cell phone and texted Omalic and Yosh. They arrived in two minutes flat, panting and sweaty from the run.

Omalic ran over to the nearest fountain to get a drink, but it was empty. He grabbed the water bottle from Neon and doused himself with what remained. Neon gave Omalic an annoyed look for finishing his water.

"So, why are we here so early?" Yosh asked.

I started my story over again, telling about the tower, the Dark Ones, and my gut feeling.

"Are you sure you're not just hallucinating?" Yosh asked. "The heat can cause some really weird stuff to—"

"For the last time, I'm not crazy," I replied. "There is something weird going on in New Kobol, and I know the Dark Ones are somehow involved. They could be building a laser to destroy us, or a huge missile, or anything, really. We don't know what it is, but we need to stop them before they do whatever they're trying to do."

In the end, we all agreed that the Dark Ones had wanted their revenge in one way or another, and we set off running down the sidewalk. I glanced at some shops, and I was desperately in need of water, especially for running so many blocks on such a hot day. They were mostly closed, however, and there were entire crowds of people milling around there until they opened back up.

That's weird, I thought to myself. *How would any store selling drinks be closed or out of stock on such a day that they could make so many sales?* However, I focused on strategies of destroying the Dark Ones in the tower. I picked up my pace and led the group around alleys and streets that seemed to go on forever until we finally reached the skyscraper. I braced myself for whatever dangers were in the building, then ran forward into it, sword held very close to my side.

After rushing through the double doors, I rammed myself into an evil-filled, death-confirming . . . reception area? I quickly stopped in my tracks. This wasn't a building of sheer terror but a normal reception area with whitewashed walls, fancy chairs, a few potted plants, and a receptionist with a tired face. The place looked more like a dentist's office than a Dark One's headquarters.

"How can I help you?" the receptionist asked in a dull, bored voice.

"We're here to see Dr. Green," Neon stepped in.

She looked at the keyboard, tapped a few keys, and looked up.

"All right. Take the elevator up to the fifty-seventh floor, room G," the receptionist replied. We all stepped into the elevator and pressed floor fifty-seven.

I made sure we were too far for the receptionist to hear, then asked Neon, "How did you do that?"

"Easy," he replied. "Dr. Green is a common name to ask for. Anyway, if there are any Dark Ones, we'll be sure to meet them on the way up."

In fact, we did meet some people going up in the elevator, but they were two businessmen with trench coats, wearing fedoras pulled over their faces. I thought it was strange because of the scorching heat outside, but they got off the elevator a few floors later. Then, I noticed something that nearly made me shriek. There were strange purple particles where the men had once stood. That was enough information for me.

We followed the businessmen. I took my sword and hit the butt of it over the two businessmen's heads. Yosh looked stricken. "Motor," he began, "what the heck are you doing?"

"Stay calm, Yosh," I said. "I know who these people really are!" I pulled off the hat of one and found . . . a horrified lab worker. He trembled in fear and got up, pushing me off him.

He ran down the stairwell yelling, "Help! Security! I've been attacked! Help!" The other worker copied the first ones' example, purple goo from a clump of jelly dripping from his coat.

We stood there for a second, motionless. It was I who finally spoke. "My Arch, I was not expecting that."

"Great, now we're wanted by the Dark Ones *and* the police," Neon said. "Come on, let's get out of here."

"No," I said, staying in the elevator.

"Motor, come on. This isn't the time to stay. Let's get out before the cops catch us," Neon commanded, sounding a bit aggravated.

"No," I repeated. "I still have that gut feeling from earlier. And it's been getting stronger ever since. I know they're here, I just know it! And if we turn back now, we could jeopardize the whole city of New Kobol. Besides, we're Knights of Archlinder. We're a team!"

Begrudgingly, the others accepted my idea, and we headed upstairs through the stairwell to avoid security from stopping us in an elevator.

As we traveled up, I could hear the water pipes in the walls nearly groaning from water pressure. I wondered how this building could have so much water when the rest of New Kobol City was bone dry. The feeling in my stomach got even heavier the more I climbed.

I was about to faint when we reached the top floor. The pipes were practically screaming in pain. As we climbed to the top, I heard a groaning that got louder. It wasn't the pipes, but it sounded like someone in intense pain. And once I heard that, I knew I had to save that person from pain and I found new strength.

I drew my sword and traveled along the hallway to the door where the victim was most likely being held. I carefully opened the door to find a black room. At once, the moaning stopped. The only thing I could now hear was my heart pounding in my ears. Omalic looked pretty scared, too, but Yosh and Neon scouted around the room. As soon as we all entered, the door shut behind us, encasing us in darkness.

"Motor?" Omalic asked. "I'm scared."

"Me too," I responded. "But we need to—wait, what was that?" There was a scuttling noise near my foot, like a bug. At once, dozens of red eyes appeared in front of us in the darkness. Neon took out his cell phone for light, revealing the three giant, red, hairy, hideous spiders in front of us. They were about as red as a fire dying out and bigger than my head. I hoped they didn't eat me.

At once, all three jumped on Neon, Omalic, and Yosh, pinning them down. I was about to make a spider shish-kabob but that would mean spearing my friends, too, so I was forced to let them be. The spiders held them down and watched me, as if waiting for me to do something.

I watched their eyes travel to the center of the room, as if directing me there. I stepped into the area they were watching, and then I smelled something burning. The lights flickered on to reveal several dashboards all manned by spiders, zombies, skeletons, creepers, and many other creatures. We also saw a huge tiled room, a huge water basin in the center of the room, and a chair at a full window that took up half of the wall. But the chair wasn't empty.

I was nearest to the chair the spiders directed me to, and as the lights revealed the room, several spiders pinned my hands to the floor. The chair appeared as if it was steaming, but it was the person in the chair that was causing the smoke. The chair swung around to show a blob the color of lava with two horns that appeared to be made from steel and an eye like a tiger's set right into the center of the blob's forehead. It seemed to be a version of the devil made out of lava.

"I have been waiting for you, Motorthud," the blob said in a deep voice.

The being didn't have a mouth, but the sentence sounded as if it was coming from the creature.

"You have been wondering about the Empire that Stewie mentioned? Well, welcome to it. Did you enjoy New Kobol?"

Many questions were flowing through my mind, so I blurted out, "Who are you?" The blob almost seemed pleased at the question and kept calm.

"Me? I am Captain Laavacan, master of the monsters ruling the terrain and keeping people scared in their homes at night. And I think I know you, hero of Vaal."

How come almost every enemy I met knew who I was?

Laavacan continued. "I hope you enjoyed New Kobol because it's the last time you'll ever see it."

I must have looked awestruck after hearing his statement. But I still managed to mock him. "What do you mean, Laava-Can't, king of the jungle?" I knew it was a bad pun and a bit cocky, but I felt the urge to say it anyway. The spiders holding my wrists tightened their grip around me.

"I wouldn't mess with me if I were you," he said. "And in detail, I will have destroyed the existence of you and New Kobol for good in exactly," he checked a clock on the wall, "fifteen minutes."

Laavacan turned back toward me. "Oh yes, in more detail. Right, right. You see that basin over there?"

I turned behind me and saw pipes coming from the ceiling into the giant tank.

"I have stored up all of New Kobol's water into there. I had to steal from stores, houses, and even sewage treatment plants, but it's all flowing into this tank. My minions and I will leave before the tank has too much water pressure and explodes, drowning you and everyone in New Kobol in its own water.

"I would stay to watch you myself, but since I'm made of lava," he touched a glass and it melted, "I'm deathly afraid of hardening and dying, so staying is out of the question. How do you feel about that, *hero*?"

Anger surged within my blood. I felt as if I were breathing out fire and heard myself growl like a wolf about to attack. Then it happened. I felt a tingling around the sword on my back and before I even realized what had happened, the spiders holding me were already on the floor, and I was holding my sword toward Laavacan. He only looked worried for a second or two but regained himself quickly.

"Quickly, attack!" he shouted. The monsters surely must not have been the sharpest swords in the armory because the spiders on Omalic, Yosh, and Neon crawled off and headed toward me. My friends each took out their weapons and started shooting the spiders and monsters coming toward me. Omalic's arrow missed, but one hit a pipe that burst a strong jet of water, pounding the spider that held him down, and the hideous beast actually disintegrated until it was just a small pile of muck.

Meanwhile, Neon was beating up the skeletons in hand-to-hand combat, Yosh was holding the zombies off with his silver blade, and Omalic was luring the lava spiders into the water, instantly killing them. Laavacan pressed a button on his chair and a chopping sound began, becoming stronger as a helicopter came swooping up from the city streets to the other side of the glass.

I couldn't let him escape and flood the city. I rushed toward the window, sword out, leaping in a perfect arc. I threw the sword into the helicopter rotors just as Laavacan was escaping. The sword landed in the rotors, denting all of them horribly, causing the helicopter to spiral out of control and head toward the ground. Laavacan was forced to leap out of the helicopter back into the building to avoid death.

After the helicopter spun out of control, I felt extremely lucky. The rotors launched my sword inside, breaking the window and heading toward all the pipes at high speed. As Omalic's arrow did to one pipe, all the pipes' jets burst toward the window, where Laavacan had just landed back inside. His one eye widened in extreme terror right before the water hit. The water nearly blinded me, so all I saw was Laavacan in terror at one moment, a black, steaming glob the next.

I went forward and kicked what was left of Laavacan. His eye, still glowing fiercely, popped out of the mound of ash. He seemed dead, but the eye still bothered me. It was then I heard his voice as if nothing had happened to him.

"I knew I should've added more defenses. Ugh, great. Now I'm just an eye. Look what you've done now, genius."

"Okay, I fixed it!" I heard Neon yell.

I turned across the room to see him near a dashboard with two words I wanted to see: Flood Cancelled. I turned my attention back toward what was left of Laavacan. I almost felt sorry for him.

"Oh, you think I'm still down, bring it on! I can still beat you just as well as I could with my body!" Right then, the guilt subsided.

I put his eye in my palm and held my sword up, aiming out the window toward a baseball park nearby.

"What are you doing?" Laavacan asked as I aimed. I threw his eye up in the air and hit it with the broad side of my sword, sending him flying down the blocks into the fields.

"Home run," I said to myself.

Chapter 13
CREATORS

FTER NEON, YOSH, OMALIC, AND I HAD RETURNED FROM THE adventure to New Kobol City, we had to go back to the actual learning part of the Academy. We were suntanned and already bored with being stuck in the classroom, even though class had only started three minutes ago. Allitode, our history teacher, walked in the classroom holding a thick book. As soon as we looked at it, everyone in the class moaned.

"Well, good morning to you too, class," he said. "But don't worry, we're only going to read a few select pages. And I've got a surprise for you today: mythology!"

The spirit in the room suddenly lifted. Mythology was easy. It was fascinating, its reenactments waste class time, and most importantly, we wouldn't be graded on it.

"Now, we're going to be reading about the Hero of Vaal," I ducked under my desk to make sure no one got suspicious of me, "tomorrow." I sat back up. "What we're going to be reading today is about the Four Thrones and Pits of Vaalbara. Can anyone tell me what they are?"

Major raised his hand.

"No bathroom humor, please," Allitode said.

Major's hand lowered.

"Any guesses?"

Leon raised his hand. "Is it the legend of the Creators of Vaal?"

"Leon, you are absolutely right," Allitode replied. "Vaal was created by Archlinder, of course, but there were also his descendants. He produced four children and told them to expand the world he had created, filled with anything anyone could imagine. So for them, Archlinder created four thrones for them and separated a bit of his soul to each of them, which are the four pits. The children could control the part of their father's soul and create whatever they desired."

"The children were three boys and a girl. The youngest son, the one who was the shyest, wanted to be stronger, so he put his father's soul into a pit and out sprang a variety of fierce creatures to guard over him, such as creepers."

I shuddered.

"And creatures you would find in the underworld. The daughter was a peacemaker, so she cast her father's soul into a different pit and out came friendly and peaceful creatures, like docile chickens and pigs. The middle son was a brave one, a lionheart, you might say. He was already content with the life he had but wanted others to experience the same joy. So he used his part of Archlinder's soul to create mankind from a pit. It wasn't evil, yet it wasn't good. It destroyed and hurt, but it built and nurtured."

Buzzy raised his hand.

"Yes, Buzzy?" Allitode asked.

"What about the other son? The oldest?"

Allitode's face fell for a moment but regained its usual smile quickly. "Well, this part of the tale is the darkest. Anyone who is faint of heart, please leave the room." No one moved. "Well, you all are knights," he said, "so here it goes. The eldest son was not content with the world. He was like the youngest son, but all the youngest wanted was to be a bit more confident. The oldest son wanted wrath. He believed that for good, there should be evil, like other religions. But he went further than that."

Allitode sat back in his chair and sighed. "He believed that there should be no one else. His pit was near empty and nothing but death radiated from it. He destroyed his siblings' creations and cast them into this pit. Every living thing he saw, he cast into the pit. Eventually, the brother even tried to kill his siblings, too. Archlinder saw this and came down to Vaal. There was an enormous final battle, and Archlinder killed his own son. The rest of the creations tossed the brother into the pit, then sealed it to create peace and live happily."

Poey asked, "What happened to the peace?"

"I was just going to discuss that," responded Allitode. "Unfortunately, the eldest brother in recent times, say a couple hundred years back, had gained some followers of his own. They eventually found his pit and found a wizard who could use dark magic to open it. The wizard, once the pit was open, sprinkled more magic dust in there, thus creating the Dark Ones."

"Wait, wait, wait," said Geo. "If the Dark Ones are from the pit, why were recent dead people in there, too?"

"Well, it's their spirits, Geo," Allitode stated. "Once someone evil dies or is killed, say a shoplifter, at least a bit of their soul travels into the pit to create more darkness. Once there is enough darkness, a creature forms from it, and the wizard uses his magic to give the dark creatures power."

At that moment, the bell rang. I then said some words that I had never said in my life: "Class is over? Dang!" During the story, I had jotted down on a piece of paper what seemed like important information to help save Vaal. I included every single thing, right down to what the Creators created. I thought that if I could find these people, they could help win the battle against the Dark Ones. At the end of the school day, I told Neon the plan in our dorm.

"I don't know, Motor," he said. "That legend must be thousands of years old. They could be dead by now, if fate allowed them death or something like that."

"Not quite," Yosh said, walking into the room. "I checked out a book on that legend a couple of weeks ago. The Creators' powers keep passing down from generation to generation. They could be anyone because it's said that the parents never tell the children who they really are."

"So basically, they couldn't help because they don't know who they are," Neon concluded.

"Yeah," replied Yosh. "A bit of a dead end. Although, sometimes there are the kids who read the legends and find out who they really are. It's pretty rare and only happens once or twice a century."

"How do you know all this stuff?" I asked.

"Internet," Yosh responded.

The internet knew a *lot*. Just then, the book on my bunk opened as if a wind had blown it open. But strangely enough, all the windows were closed.

I went over to examine what had happened. I saw the blank page. I wrote:

Sorry I haven't written in a while. Defeated a Dark Overlord, ruler of monsters. Ever heard of Legend of Thrones and Pits? Sounds like Creators could help me. RSVP ASAP.

Shiro and Furry immediately responded:

Great for the takeover of the Dark Overlord! Legend of Thrones and Pits sounds familiar, but not too sure where it's from. A bit busy with other things at the moment. TTYL, Shiro.

"What'd they say?" Neon asked.

"Shiro said she didn't know what the legend was, but she somehow felt she knew of it. I'm not entirely sure. But anyway, she was busy with something else but she didn't explain."

"So, basically no help?" Yosh asked.

"Yosh, stop reading Motor's mind!" Neon said, covering my ears, causing us all to crack up.

Yosh's eyes suddenly lit up. "Guys, there might actually be a way to see if the legend is real." We all inched closer to Yosh, listening intently. "If the Dark Ones captured even two of the Creators, then we would all most likely be dead. But we aren't! That means there are still the other three good Creators!" At this point, Yosh had a mad look in his eyes and rubbed his hands. "If we could just capture and harness the Creators' powers, we could obliterate the Dark Ones and everyone who mistook us! Muhahahahahaha."

Neon slapped Yosh across the face with the back of his hand.

"Sorry," Yosh said. "Hunger sometimes makes me insane. Heh heh. We could track down people that look—"

"Strange?" I suggested.

"Already on it!" said Omalic, walking into the dorm carrying what looked like a cross between a toy tank and a doll. He then set down the tank and pulled out a sheet of paper from his pocket with a list of names on it.

"This is every person that has appeared strange or weird to me or anyone else since I came to the Academy," said Omalic.

I recognized a few names like Lewis, Tilly, and Ian, but there was one that was unfamiliar to me.

"Silverstealth?" I asked. I remembered seeing a new kid around the Academy but never caught his name. All I remembered was a silver helmet with shining, bright blue eyes underneath.

"Yes, often known for being shy or hiding in corridors."

"Omalic, that's not weird, he's just shy. The only reason Motor doesn't recognize him may be because he arrived a week after him," Yosh suggested. "So we can scratch that one off the list," he said, taking a pen in hand and making a line through Silver. Then he made a strange face.

"Omalic," he said, "why did you put *my* name on this list?"

"Whoops! Must've been a typo or something," Omalic said, taking the list and pen from Yosh and scribbling something out.

"Seriously though, guys," Neon said, "We've got work to do."

◆　　◆　　◆

And the next day, there I was, crouching around a corner spying on Ian. After we all agreed to spy on the strange people in the Academy the previous day, we had all been assigned a possible Creator heir. So far, Ian wasn't doing much. He mainly texted and occasionally waved to a guy or two.

This really wasn't worth it. My knees were falling asleep, and Ian showed no signs of strangeness whatsoever. It was when I felt a cold hand tap me on the shoulder that I actually reacted to anything.

I gave a small yelp and leaped forward as I recoiled. I then realized it was just my secrecy teacher, Loiwol.

"Spying?" he asked. I nodded. It seemed only when I was busy watching someone he could show up and read my mind.

"Well, you're doing a fantastic job," he said. I raised my hand to shoo him away to regain my focus on Ian. He nodded, showing he understood, and strolled back into his classroom without a sound. I looked back at Ian, almost wishing I had gotten someone who could do something interesting. I had been nodding off for quite a bit now.

A couple of minutes later, I got what I was looking for. In mid-text, Ian froze and his phone dropped to the ground. He started to float into the air, as if pulled by a tractor beam. A strange look appeared in his eyes, and it turned into a green destructive laser in the next moment. He let loose a bloodcurdling shriek and a giant UFO swooped down to the Academy window and started firing missiles toward the building. This was the weird I was looking for!

I drew my sword in case Ian became too hostile and started to advance toward the monster that was previously a fellow student. But I was stopped by an orange paw, clamped tightly down on my shoulder. "Motorthud? Motorthud!" it kept saying and started shaking me back and forth. My vision then felt dizzy and sick. I felt something pulling me into darkness. "Motor! Motor!" The tiger kept yelling.

"No!" I said, shoving away the great orange mass holding me down. I started kicking the creature until I heard Neon's voice emanate from the tiger. "Motor! Ow! What are you doin—ow!" I looked around at the scene of alien attack on the

Academy, and suddenly, I snapped back to reality.

All the students were staring as I was kicking Neon, who was lying on the floor. The UFO outside the window had turned out to be a small bird knocking itself against the glass. I stopped my foot and returned it to the ground.

"Ow, I'm fine, everything's good people! Nothing to see here!" Neon said, getting back up. He must've been the tiger. A few seconds went by, and everyone soon dispersed.

"Motor, what were you doing?" he asked.

"I have no idea, but Ian was floating, and UFOs were . . . and a tiger . . ." I stumbled over my words.

"Motor, the—erm—tiger. Were you kicking him?"

"Yes," I replied astonishingly. How could he have known?

"Well," he said, "It looks like you might have been a sleep-fighter. Explains why your bed is usually a mess in the morning."

"I guess," I replied. I wasn't quite sure how to react to finding out I was a sleep-fighter.

"Nothing weird about Ian?" Neon asked, brushing dust off his shirt.

"Only in my dreams," I said. "He's just kind of normal. Not bad in real life, only bad when you're using this," I said, holding up the list of weird people in the Academy Omalic had given to me. I crossed out Ian's name.

"So, anything weird with your guy?" I asked.

"Tilly? No, he's just kind of random."

My eyes lit up at the possibility of the Creator's heir.

"But only in conversations. Not much else," Neon said. An insect flew through the air and landed on Neon's neck. He slapped it, suddenly flinching.

"Hey, can I see that?" he asked, taking the list. He scribbled out Tilly's name furiously, then walked away.

"A waste of a couple of hours of my life, along with that stupid bug that just bit me," he said. "I had a sparring session with Poey that I've been waiting weeks for, and I had to cancel for this," he grumbled, holding up the source of our lost time.

"Well, hopefully Yosh got something from his guy," I said.

"Yeah, I guess you're right. But if he didn't, I'm gonna give Omalic a piece of my mind!"

We walked up to the cafeteria but quickly ran under a table as a bolt of lightning struck near the building. It somehow went from a nice, sunny morning to pouring rain. It was hard to even speak and be heard over the storm. Thankfully, the teachers had already rolled out the tarps and the whole area was covered from the storm. Neon and I got our lunches and sat down at a table to wait and see if Omalic and Yosh had come up with anything.

It was a little while later until Omalic came up the stairs with a pleased smirk on his face. "Well? Did you find someone odd?" Neon asked.

"Okay, Motor. First, wipe the strawberry off your face. You look ridiculous," Omalic said. I grabbed a napkin and wiped off the mess.

"Second, I lost Yosh. I have no idea where he is! He could have been run over by an elephant or worse." Omalic trembled. "He could've been taken by vampire pirates! Oh no! What should I do? What should I do? What—"

During Omalic's frenzied runaround, Neon had taken out his phone and gotten to his inbox. "Omalic?" Neon said. "You might want to look at this." He handed the phone, chuckling, to Omalic.

Omalic gave a strange look and read Yosh's message aloud. "Hey, Neon! Ditching Omalic to watch that new movie, *Swords and Shins!* Feel bad for you there!" Neon started laughing hysterically.

Omalic angrily slammed the phone on the table. "Why that no good—" he started, but Neon cut in.

"Come on, Omalic, it's pretty funny, you gotta admit."

"I guess," said Omalic, now grinning. "Oh! Almost forgot. I found a random guy!"

"You did?" Neon and I both leaned in to listen in interest.

"He's right over there," Omalic said, pointing toward the Academy's humungous forest. I scanned the area until I saw a figure in a green outfit prancing around in the storm.

"Omalic, that's Sonic!" Neon said. "Everyone knows he's crazy!" Neon's anger was coming back and stronger than the first time. "You think you can just waste my time looking for a lost cause?" Neon was practically shouting now and edging Omalic back into a corner. I saw fear in Omalic's eyes.

"Well, you know what?" Neon forcefully yelled at Omalic.

I needed to stop this somehow.

"I think you're just a puny little—"

"Wait!" I cried at Neon. He turned around, a bit surprised, but still full of anger.

"What is it? Another waste of my time?" Omalic was slowly approaching us from the corner.

"No, it's not a time waster. It's . . . um . . ." I quickly looked around for anything to stop Neon from choking Omalic.

"I swear, if this wastes one more second of my life, I'm going to—"

My eyes finally settled on the forest.

"There!" I said, pointing through the trees.

"We've already seen Sonic. He's not much," Neon reminded me.

"Well, it's time I introduce you guys to a friend. Come on." I edged down the stairs, Neon ahead of me. Before disappearing into the lower story, I looked at Omalic, still holding back tears in the corner of the cafeteria Neon had backed him into.

"Coming?" I whispered to him, too silent for Neon to hear.

He wiped his eyes, saying "Sure," with a little sadness in his voice. I knew I needed something to cheer him up. I couldn't look at Omalic like this. It somehow made me feel depressed.

"Nothing will make you feel better?" I asked.

He quietly whimpered, "Nothing."

I knew that wouldn't be true. I went up to the cafeteria and got an ice pop for him. As soon as I came back, I set it in front of him.

He stared down at it for a second. But I saw something happy in his eyes as he tore open the wrapping with a huge smile on his face. He finished the treat in a matter of seconds, red smudged all over his mouth.

"Okay, maybe some things make me feel better," Omalic said, laughing.

"Come on!" An angry voice yelled from downstairs.

I'd almost forgotten about Neon during Omalic's brief bout of depression.

"Coming!" I yelled back to him.

"Let's go," I said to Omalic. "We have a weird guy to see." Right before heading to the stairs, I looked at Omalic. "And you might want to take a napkin with you." I pointed to Omalic's face.

"Nah, I'm fine," he said, licking his lips clean. Then we headed down the stairs, into the rain outside.

Chapter 14
THE WIND AT THE GRAVE

WE HEADED OUTSIDE INTO THE RAIN, THE WATERED GRASS squeaking beneath our feet. I walked toward the forest, hoping I could get some help. I didn't know exactly what I was doing; I was just protecting Omalic against Neon's anger by distracting Neon from possibly doing something that could affect all of our friendships.

I circled around to the back of the building near the hospital where I had first been treated for allergies to the dark phoenix feather. I looked past the small building into the trees and gulped. I was still having nightmares about the event that occurred in there only weeks ago.

I retraced my steps from then, following a small dirt path, not too worn from travelers. I could see why. It was getting scary as I walked deeper into the trees. Most light disappeared, and the rain pounded against the leaves.

I closed my eyes, trying to get to the last point. I kept randomly trudging around until I didn't feel the tall grass brushing against my legs anymore. I opened my eyes, looking into the familiar clearing. Neon piped up again.

"We just came here to see a graveyard? I swear, I will—"

I tuned him out. I looked until I found the stone with the small text on it. I checked both sides, finding the nightmare-causing image on the back with the two glaring eyes staring into one's soul. I brushed my hand against the face, the stone turning blue with a mysterious glow that I had already known. Whatever Neon was saying when I stopped listening got caught in his throat as a shadowy figure rose from the ground in front of the grave.

As Neon went bug-eyed and Omalic looked up in awe, I stood calmly next to the ghost I had met as he stretched from the grass.

"Who dares wake Whiteisa, the—" He stopped ranting about himself and stared down at me. "Oh, hello Motorthud!" he said casually.

I waved back at him.

"It's nice that finally, someone comes for a visit! Everyone else gets scared away!" He had a smile on his face. He looked over at a paralyzed Neon and Omalic.

"Who are these two?" he asked.

"You see, Whiteisa," I explained, "these are my friends, Omalic and Neon. And we were looking for some help."

Omalic and Neon waved at him, an expression of mixed terror still on Neon's face.

"It's okay, guys, we're cool," I said. Neon no longer looked angry but was still slightly shocked.

Whiteisa looked around, as if searching for someone or something important. His eyes settled on a spot a small space away from Neon. Whiteisa sprang forward in the air like a cat, landing on the ground with his hands cupped like he captured the baseball game's winning catch.

"I got it," he said, opening his hands to reveal a black bug with purple dragonfly wings. The creature was at least an inch long, with a tube where its mouth should be. Whiteisa looked with disgust at what was in his hands.

"Ira Cimex," he spat out. "The Dark Ones have stepped up their game."

I could see anger in his eyes.

"Ira what?" Omalic asked. I had no idea what Whiteisa was talking about either; neither Omalic nor I had seen the thing in our lives.

"It doesn't matter. Anyway, why did you come here? I know it wasn't for just a visit."

"You see," I started, "we've been trying to spy on other students at the Academy to see if any of them could be a Creator to help us defeat the Dark Ones."

Whiteisa listened intently.

"So we were having the hardest times spying. Always getting interrupted or attracting too much attention to ourselves. Since you are a ghost, we were thinking—"

"Yes!" Whiteisa immediately responded, cheering.

"We haven't even told you what it is yet," Neon said.

"I don't care. I just really want to be able to get out of the ground and actually see the Academy for myself! I've explored a bit at movies, but this will be interesting!"

The whole situation was out of our way now. I felt pretty good, getting more time and making Whiteisa happy.

"You can turn invisible, right?" I asked him.

To demonstrate, he went over to a tree. He was there for a second, but then it seemed like he dissolved into the tree. I felt a tap on my shoulder and turned around to see him there, smiling.

"Okay. I'll start investigating the Academy while you guys go back and keep us safe! Bye now!" Whiteisa said, floating toward the Academy, turning invisible as soon as he left the clearing.

I could hear him giggling with glee on the way out.

◆　　◆　　◆

With Whiteisa handling the spying, we relaxed a little. When we got back inside, we decided to do a little research. I looked in the old books section in the farthest corner of the library. I figured that if Whiteisa *had* known about it, and even Neon *didn't*, it must be in a book unused for ages.

I scanned the titles: *How to Avoid the Black Death*, *Remsen's Almanac, 1834 Edition*, and a tractor safety manual. I eventually found *Dark One Bugs and Other Disasters* right behind a copy of a video game booklet. I flipped through and found a picture of the bug from earlier, right along with a description:

> *Ira Cimex: Latin for "Anger Bug." This mosquito-like creature of the Dark Ones injects the chemical* plumenitorium *into the host's body, making the host uncontrollably violent and impatient. After injecting the victim, the insect hides where it will least likely be found—in the host's hair. The only way to get rid of the Ira Cimex is to scare it out of the host. To kill it, you must, without touching it, smash it between two surfaces.*

Neon peered over my shoulder, reading the entry with me. "That explains how I must've gotten so angry," he said.

"And how Whiteisa killed it," Omalic said. "He smashed it between his hands, but he's a ghost! Hopefully, that won't affect him."

"Now I know what the Dark Ones were trying to do!" I said. "They injected Neon with that plumenitury stuff, trying to break our relationship and leaving us stranded with us not able to help one another to overcome our differences!"

Neon and Omalic stared at me.

"Okay, Yosh has been teaching me psychology, but it's only for trying to get my memory back!"

It was somewhat true. Yosh had been reading psychology books aloud to himself late at night, not allowing me to fall asleep and forcing me to listen to him until the next morning.

"I knew I should have bought earplugs," I said to myself, remembering the event.

We returned upstairs to our room to work on our homework from the other day while waiting for Yosh and Whiteisa to arrive back from whatever they were doing. I was on number five of secrecy homework, *What would you use to hollow out a book?*, when Yosh walked back in with bags of popcorn, his hand in his pocket, and a big grin on his face.

"Yosh, it may look like it's heaven to you, but we're just doing homework, nothing amazing about it," Neon said firmly.

"You guys know how I was at the movies earlier?" Yosh asked, ignoring Neon's comment.

We nodded.

"Well, since I was the 746th person there, I got free tickets for another time!" Yosh exclaimed, pulling four tickets out of his pocket.

We all jumped up as if someone poured ice down our backs and ran over to Yosh to look at the tickets. "Does this make up for the 'incident' that happened last week, guys?"

We all nodded, not paying much attention to his question as we drooled over the tickets to the greatest movie of the season. The "incident" Yosh was referring to last week was . . . oh, he made us swear we wouldn't tell. All I can say is, he owed us one.

At that moment, I looked over at the popcorn Yosh had brought back with him and saw that it still seemed to be popping. It was moving in clumps and much higher than it would have normally. Then a clump went up in the air and disappeared. As soon as I noticed, Omalic started staring at the popcorn, too. He nudged Neon with his elbow, pointing at the strange food. We were all astounded, but Yosh was busy blabbering on about something having to do with some of the great scenes. Eventually, he noticed we were no longer paying attention.

"What are you guys so mesmerized about?" he asked, turning to where we were looking. Just then, Whiteisa came out of his invisibility as he was shoveling another handful of popcorn into his mouth. Yosh looked right at Whiteisa, widened his eyes, and slowly, gingerly, put out his hand. Yes, Yosh, one of the most easily frightened people I have ever met, saw a ghost and went to shake his hand. If those psychology books helped him do that, I'd have to listen to him read aloud more.

Whiteisa, just as shocked as I was at Yosh's act, slowly went over, placing Yosh's hand in his own and shook. But quickly, he returned to his usual inflated ego.

"Why are you not trembling at the great ghost of Whiteisa?" His booming voice shook the beds.

"I've been noting paranormal activity here and expected something to turn up. Besides, I've read about you before in books. You aren't very—" Yosh stopped as soon as he saw the hostility in Whiteisa's eyes.

"Very well-described in the books. Much stronger in person," Yosh said, with the face of someone trying to avoid harsh punishment. So much for that random confidence boost of his.

"Did you find anything?" Neon asked Whiteisa.

Yosh gave me a confused look. I quickly explained to him how we wanted to find the Creator possibilities.

"Gotcha, gotcha," Yosh said, nodding.

"So, *did* you find anything?" Neon asked again.

"Well," said the forgotten king, "I saw a chicken strutting around."

"I mean, did you find anything that was linked to the Creators?" Neon spoke down to him, obviously annoyed.

"Hold your jet engines, I'm getting to that! So I also found someone on the grounds, and let's just say he was looking for you," he said, pointing toward me.

"What do you mean he was—" but I stopped mid-sentence as something rolled through the door. It was a small children's toy; the monkey that banged cymbals together, although this one's hat had a strange marking—a lapis blue and silver kind of mask. Neon knew what it was immediately.

"Head for the window!" he shouted, jumping past Omalic, who was intently studying the item.

"What for?" Yosh asked.

"Just hurry so—"

Whatever else Neon said was drowned out by the toy starting to bang the instruments together. Then its mouth lowered and a purple fog sprayed out of the mouth. I saw Whiteisa float through the wall and hurry back into the woods. The toy's head started to spin around, filling the room with the intoxicating spray. All of a sudden, I couldn't hear anything. It felt like there were goosebumps all over me. Everything became blurry, like a dream.

"Yes, it is just a dream," a feminine voice said, softly. "Just go back to sleep. Back to sleep . . ."

"Back to sleep," I mumbled, closing my eyes as the stench entered my nostrils. My head hit the floor, and I felt darkness close around me.

Chapter 15
Interrogation

WHEN I WAS KNOCKED OUT, I FELT LIKE I WAS TRAPPED inside my own body. I could think fine, but I couldn't move, not even blink. I could tell I was recovering from the toxic gas, but not fast enough. I couldn't handle being trapped.

My body is too small a space, and I'm—well, let's just say, easily claustrophobic.

Slowly, feeling returned to my now conscious body. It was a tight and dark place, and I was moving. I could hear an engine and felt that I was lying on some kind of cloth. I sniffed the air but quickly regretted it, as the stench of sweat greeted me. I tried to move, but I was squashed between loads of fabric on top of me, and the cloth was on a cold, metal surface.

I slowly regained my senses, and the engine I heard was pretty loud. I felt something sticky and cold around my mouth, maybe duct tape. My wrists and ankles were bound together by a strong rope that tightened when I moved. Since I was helpless, all I could do was feel and listen to the engine as we headed to our unknown destination.

Eventually, in the situation I was in, with nothing to do, I decided to take a quick nap. I closed my eyes, and I was instantly asleep, tired from the breathtaking events. But when I fell asleep, it wasn't just blackout the whole time. I had a dream.

First, it was dark, and two figures were floating up. Then it got brighter and I saw that the figures were underwater, swimming faster and faster in a panic. I couldn't see the unknown threat.

Then the image cleared up, and I saw they were two girls wearing almost the exact same outfit. I heard a shot, and a harpoon, still attached by a rope, blasted past the two girls. More harpoons followed, missing them by only inches.

The harpoons stopped shooting. I saw relief in the girls' faces as they headed up to the water's surface, only yards away. Then, a harpoon snaked up and struck one of the girl's ankles and wrapped its rope around it, pulling her down to the darkness of the ocean. The image cleared up more, and I could see perfectly. The girl being pulled down was thrashing around, her brown hair getting thrown around in the ocean current. She reached up to the girl nearest the surface, the one with red hair. They looked familiar to me. I saw her reach out, her fingers almost touching the captured girl's.

Then the brown-haired girl got pulled down, out of the red-haired girl's reach. I saw her eyes full of emotion, trying to get back to her friend. Then, I saw her open her mouth. Bubbles came out. Then my vision faded. I tried to listen more, but I was somehow out of range. All I heard was the red-haired girl yelling, "Shiro!"

I opened my eyes, instantly struggling to try and save the girl, not caring about the pain as the rope cut tighter around my wrists. Then I realized I had woken up, and the experience was just a dream. A dream reminding me of Furry and Shiro. I sure hoped they were all right.

Eventually, I felt the plane descend, hitting the tarmac like a hammer on a nail, causing the bag I was in to jump up and slam me back down against the metal surface. I heard the back of the plane open, and a high pitched, male voice. It wasn't a pirate voice, but it was city-like.

"Eh, was sure smart takin' the kid with the Academy laundry, huh? Capture an' torture, with the way those teens sweat! Not bad for the rookie, eh Boomer?"

A deeper voice, presumably Boomer's, replied, "It's been done before. Trust me, this company is one of those oddball jobs, never just plain old customer service. Nope, gotta make toys, weapons, weapons that are toys. Basically, you did a regular job, Gim."

I heard the sacks being unloaded, and I started to think. Putting me in with the laundry explained the smell, but what did these guys want with me? And even though this was probably the place that made the weapon toys that captured me, where exactly was this place? It could've been New Kobol or the jungle. Anything was possible.

My train of thought was interrupted when the bag I was in started to move. l got lifted in the air for half a second, then dropped back on the metal like a rock. I heard Gim's voice again after he kicked a spot on the bag. Unfortunately, that spot happened to be where my face was.

"'Ey Boomer!" he said. "Either the boy's in this one or this is the XXXL load! Come and help me lift this, would'ja?"

Judged by how quickly the bag was lifted back up, and without any panting or second attempts, Boomer must've been the strong one of the two, making me rethink any chances of trying to escape mid-carry. Then, the bag stopped moving. I heard Gim rummaging around in his pockets, mumbling to himself, and then a metallic voice.

"Member recognized. Gim Banner: Rookie, weakling, working in kidnapping. Enjoy the rest of your day at GoldenSneak Industries. PS: Your work break was 38.5792001 seconds overdue, your pay for now until closing will be docked. Thank you." Another beep issued, and I heard a door glide open.

"Hate that dang machine," said Gim. "Watches you every second, make that nano-second. And it even judges you!"

"Well," explained Boomer, "it's gonna be worth it. Golden-Sneak runs pretty smoothly, and this—" he said, shaking the bag "—is gonna make the boss super happy, and hopefully gonna get us a pay raise."

They walked in silence the rest of the way, only stopping at a few doors to take out their key cards, where I had the luxury of hearing Gim whine more. The deeper we went into the factory, I heard more beeping and machinery than at the entrance. I assumed that the boss of an industry that has such advanced and complicated work robots needed extra protection.

We finally reached a highly protected door. They set the bag on the ground and followed the computer's instructions: "Put hand on pad. Good. Put foot on pad. Good. Put eye to scanner. Good. Put tongue on pad. Good. Workers identified. Now, put cleaning wipe on tongue, you disgusting globs of carbon."

I heard the doors slide apart and smelled a room like an old lady's house. Once the doors closed themselves, there were no sounds of machinery, just a foot tapping on solid steel.

"We brought him, boss," said Boomer, the deeper-voiced one.

I then heard a voice that sounded average but made you want to obey him. Powerful, yet kind, and not demanding. Almost businesslike. It sounded somewhat familiar. "Good. Set him on that chair."

I was dropped down and heard the two men leave. I heard a whir in machinery that came down from the ceiling and come close to me until it stopped. Then, the pressure of the bag holding me in loosened more and more, until the bag came untied and slipped out from under me. I saw two robot hands hanging inches above my head, making their way back into the ceiling with the sack. I threw down the rest of the clothes that I had nearly suffocated in.

I observed my surroundings. I was in a cold, steel chair attached to the floor. There were mirrored walls all around me, like a small ballet studio. Across from me, on the other side of a metal table also melted into the floor, a somewhat tall, dark figure sat with his hands tapping on the table. There was a dark screen dividing his side of the room from mine, so I couldn't see his face, only his shadow, shining from the light behind him.

"So Motor," he said, "what brings you here?" He chuckled at his own little joke.

I was angry. "Your henchmen, you dirty little—"

"Whoa, whoa! Settle down, I'm not the bad guy. Although, I can see why you think so. You see, I just need to ask you a few questions."

Fearing he was a Dark One, I jumped up out of the chair and reached behind me. But my sword wasn't there. I removed my scabbard and examined it, but no weapon was there. I continued groping around for anything as the figure watched.

"Yes, your sword. That had to be removed after you got knocked out. We feared you could become dangerous, as by what your friends told." I instantly stopped looking and stared at him. "Ah yes, your friends. Don't worry about them, they've already been in here and came out in one piece. As I said, I just need to ask a few questions, and then you may leave."

"With my friends?" I asked.

"Yes. Now, where shall I begin?" As he ruffled through what appeared to be a folder, I sat back down, in case my attitude affected my time of departure.

"Okay, first question," he said. "Who are your best friends?"

"Neon, Omalic, and Yosh," I answered, not missing a beat.

He nodded. "Mmhm, okay. Where do you live?"

"The Academy, as a Knight of Archlinder."

A buzzing sound, like one that was issued when the wrong answer was chosen on a game show, came from the walls.

He rested his elbow on the desk. "I don't think you're telling me the complete truth," he said, sounding a little annoyed.

What could I have not been right about? Then I remembered something that Furry said *And never, ever, ever, ever say anything at* all *about me, Shiro, or Ida.*

I decided to say, "What do you mean?"

I heard some beeps and more whirring, and I felt the cold metal I was previously sitting on become extremely hot. I jumped off in surprise as a television swooped down from the ceiling. The figure behind the screen looked very serious.

"Do not mess with me, Motorthud. And don't forget that I run a huge business industry, big enough to have certain technology . . ." He fingered a remote in his hands and flicked it towards the television, which flicked on instantly.

And, amazed, I watched all the memories I had, right from when I woke up in that field, including my thoughts. I sat there in shock, not believing that this kind of technology was possible and that someone could get my entire life from a chair. I could tell he was enjoying this, right up until the part where I was in the fight with Stewie.

He paused the monitor and set down the remote. He sat back in his chair, sighing. "Well," he said, "based on this scenario, and the strength of your relationships, I'm going to say it: You need my help."

I just stared at him. I didn't know whether to thank him for the help or feel insulted that I needed "help." Instead, I asked the only question left on my mind. "Who are you?"

He sat back in his chair, turning over the remote in his hand. "I knew you'd ask that one way or another. Allow me to introduce myself." His thumb jabbed down on a button, causing the screen in the room to lift. He had black gloves and lapis blue sleeves and leggings, covered by a silver and chain mail warrior pelt. His helmet was made of steel, with a small opening that allowed breathing but concealed the face. The helmet's eye holes glowed the color of the ocean.

"Allow me to introduce myself as Silverquick."

I stared openmouthed. "But you're—"

"The exact same as my son Silverstealth? Yes, yes, I am. I am the CEO of GoldenSneak Industries, a multi-trillionaire in selling weaponry against the Dark Ones."

Now I remembered the voice. I had heard Loi watching a commercial for a toy helicopter that carried a bomb, voiced by CEO Silverquick from GoldenSneak. But I still had to know why this guy wanted me, and what kind of game he was playing.

I set my elbows down on the table. "Why did you bring me here?"

He didn't seem surprised at the question. "My son had been noticing you were acting strange recently—said something about watching others, chatting in private, and so on. So he wrote a letter to me, and I sent him back a bio-scanner and tracked you some of the time."

It disturbed me that Silverstealth would've been tracking and stalking me, but I let his dad carry on.

"He noticed you went off into the woods, and sometimes, another unknown life form would appear, going through walls of the preset coordinates. He thought he was in danger, so I sent him that toy that got you knocked out and some of my best hit men. Once he heard the unknown person, your ghost friend, judging by your memories, he threw down the weapon and here you are."

After scanning the unsettling events several times in my head, I returned to what Silverquick had said earlier. "What exactly did you mean by, 'I need your help'?"

"Well, judging by the commitment to your friends, and the terribly nasty fight," he shuddered, "to survive, you must have intricate weaponry on your side, especially if you, the hero of Vaal, are up against the entire Dark Ones' army! Fortunately, being a trillionaire has its perks, so I can provide to you some of the best I have. You know, because I've got *cash*."

Silverquick wasn't going to win any humility awards anytime soon.

As he explained more and went over some of my memories that played back on the tape, I focused on the irony of the situation. When Omalic thought Silver was being strange, Silver actually thought we were being strange. And it turned out that we didn't even need to discover who the Creator was to get help from someone.

"So, want to come and see around the factory? We have a few weapons I think you'll like!" He pressed another button on the remote, unlocking the door behind me. We walked out, taking a look at a giant processing plant, featuring almost anything anyone could ever need or imagine. While still gaping, I examined some of the factory lines with Silverquick. I picked up what looked like a small oval of orange on one piece of machinery.

"Don't drop that!" yelled Silverquick, quickly taking the object out of my hand and putting it inside a nearby glass case, sealing it shut. "You see that bug in there?" he asked, pointing at the dangerous object. I looked again and saw it was a bug trapped in the orange amber. "There is a highly dangerous swarm of wasps in there, all making up that shape."

I saw that the bug figure was moving, but not as a whole; different parts moved independently of one another.

We walked into a secluded lab area safeguarded with the hardest lock of all time: the slide puzzle. I could tell it was a lab from the smell of ammonia and the frequent explosions behind metal doors. I looked up at something covered in a huge tarp, three stories tall. "What's that?" I asked Silver's dad, pointing at the mystery.

"Let's just say, SpiderStealth is for a rainy day, or as the scientists said, a rainy *dooms*day."

I shuddered to think of whatever was beneath that tarp. One thing was for sure when looking at the size of it: I did *not* want to be a Dark One.

After Silverquick and I looked at some more items in the lab, we went to the break room, where Omalic, Neon, and Yosh were leaning back sipping coffee. I also saw my sword in the corner, unharmed. I turned back to Silverquick. "Thanks for the help," I said.

"Oh, it was nothing. Plus, I'm going to leave you with this," he said, putting the amber through a loop and around my neck like a necklace. I felt the buzzing against my chest, my heart almost beating in time to the alien pulse. "I figured you could probably handle it if anything pops up."

I looked up to Silverquick. "Thanks for everything."

"No problem! Just *bee* careful with it!"

I suddenly wanted to slap him, but resisted the urge.

He got us back on a jet to the Academy (with seats!), and we chatted on the way.

"Did you see that auto-targeting flash bomb?" asked Omalic. "And the self-replicating grenades? So insane!"

"Omalic, I didn't know you liked weapons so much," said Yosh. "After all, you seem to mainly use just your bow and arrow."

Yosh had a point. I had seen him thumbing through some artillery magazines and knew he could afford it based on the jet his dad gave to him, but I had only seen him with his old-fashioned bow.

"It's mainly just for sentimental reasons. Originally my mom's." He looked into the sky, silently saying, "Arch bless her soul."

However, I had noticed. "Why's that? What happened to her?" I asked.

Omalic looked directly at me, remorse on his face.

"Motor!" Neon hissed, grimacing, shaking his head and sliding a finger across his throat.

"No, no guys, it's fine," Omalic said. "It all happened a long time ago, anyway. We were camping in the Archirondack Mountains. The Dark Ones were spreading, so we decided to take a little family vacation." He gently laughed. "What we didn't realize was that we were only a few miles from one of their base camps, and they were planning an invasion that night."

"When my parents heard the distinctive creaking, they ushered me into a cave and told me to stay silent. But before she ran off, my mom left me with her spare bow and a small quiver of arrows. I stayed huddled in that cave until far into the next morning. I'm not even sure if I slept that night." His voice was getting shaky.

"But what she told me before was that if I ever feel scared or frightened, I should just laugh it off." He laughed cautiously again, as if to assure everything was alright. We all stared at him.

"Omalic . . . I . . ." Yosh started, but Omalic got up.

"I've gotta use the restroom," he said, speed-walking to the bathroom. The plane was silent for the rest of the flight.

After we recovered from the incredibly dark flight and left Omalic on his own for a bit, Neon, Yosh and I ran to our dorm to chill out. I fingered the amber orb in my hands, admiring the movement of the creatures. But then I realized something important that I had to do before relaxing. I jumped off my bunk and made my way down the hall to Silver's dorm.

Chapter 16
ALLIANCE

I WALKED ACROSS THE HALL TO A DORM WHICH I NOW KNEW belonged to a trillionaire's son. I knocked on the door three times with no response. I put my ear against the door, hearing the whirs and beeps of the sophisticated technology that I now knew only GoldenSneak Industries could acquire. I knocked again. This time there was a response.

"Uh, Silver's not in right now!" said Silver in a false voice of his roommate, Ecao. "In fact, I think he left forever."

"Silver, I know that's you!" I said. I heard a soft "Drat!" on the other side of the door. But the door still didn't move.

"It's Motor! I just met your dad. I wanna talk to you!" I whispered through the wood.

The door opened a crack, one of Silver's eyes poking out. He decided I had to go through a check, though.

"What's my dad's name?" he asked.

"Silverquick, CEO of GoldenSneak Industries."

"What does he look like?"

"Look in a mirror, he looks like you."

"Any questions from you?"

"Yes, why does your family ask so many questions?"

He chuckled, fully opening the door. "Come in, come in. Sorry about the mess," he said, indicating a table on the side of the room where stacks upon stacks of blueprints lay. It looked like the standard Academy room, but with some purple window blinds, a desk in the corner, and several robots scampering around the room.

"This is amazing," I said. "How do you hide them from your roommates?"

"It's easy," he said. "I just have to press this button and . . ." He pressed a button on his desk and the cluttered blueprints folded themselves up into a neat stack. The desk legs flew into the desk's bottom and folded back into the wall. A panel slid over the exposed bottom of the table. The robots previously all over the room went under the nearest bed and turned themselves off. They hid under the bed—no cool cloaking device.

"I can explain the robots," Silver said. "No one checks under there, ever, so there's no need to hide them even more. I sometimes think that Ecao's bed had a student under it when the term started."

"Cool, cool. Anyway, I wanted to apologize for 'apparently' seeming weird around you," I said, trying to be evidently passive-aggressive.

"It's okay," he replied. "I'm sorry for putting you in a laundry sack, sending you by plane to an obscure location, and putting photos of you onto the internet where you had makeup that I put on your face when you were unconscious."

"Apology accep—wait, what was that last one?"

He looked uncomfortable. "So, what's the reason you came over here? It wasn't just to steal blueprints, was it?" he said, menacingly pulling out a remote.

I stepped back a bit. "No, it was about something else. Your dad knows this now, so I ought to pass it on to you. I'm—"

"The hero of Vaal? Knew it," he said, making his bed and reacting as if I had just said the forecast for today.

I then remembered that Silver had been listening in on our conversations and heard one of us mention it, or he got a call from his dad pretty quickly. Either explanation was possible.

"Right, right," I said, passing it off as if I hadn't been surprised. "Also, I came here to ask. Do you want to join Omalic, Yosh, Neon, and me?"

He perked up in surprise. He sat down on the bed, shaking his head to himself.

"Motor," he said. "I really didn't expect this. I mean, maybe an apology and possibly some baked goods but proposition of an alliance? Are you serious about this? Me? Join you guys? I'm just a wimp, and you guys are brave and heroic, and the only form of combat I've ever done is on a game! I don't know if I can do this." He went back to shaking his head in his arms.

I sat down on the bed and patted him on the back." That's not all true," I said to him. "We all have weaknesses. And you aren't a wimp. Take the time you tried and captured me, for example. You have the strength to strategize. The way you observed from afar, knew when to attack. That was awesome! And by the way, how did you get Whiteisa to meet you and talk to you?"

He sat up. "Easy," he said, with more confidence in his voice. "I just set up cameras and saw you going in there. Then on the bio-scanner, I saw something fly out of the woods. Also, my dad got me a working poltergeist backpack for Halloween. It's in the chest," he said, pointing toward a chest in the corner marked *Silver's Stuff.*

I encouraged him again. "See? Strategic! I never even knew you were watching us! That's why you'd be perfect with us."

But he seemed suspicious again. "This isn't just so you can get some of our money? Because I've had plenty of charmers who tried to come and do that, and you don't want to know what happened to them."

He started to scare me a bit. "No, dude, it's not about your dad's money. In fact, you could've kidnapped me like you did before with a straw and box! Plus, what you just did to me right there, you're pretty threatening in some situations."

He beamed up at me now. "Really?"

I nodded.

It took him a minute to weigh the scales and charts in his head. But after careful plotting and consideration, he found a point. "Motor, I would like you to know that . . ."

Excitement welling up inside me. I would finally have a good team! Major would fear us, and we could conquer the Dark Ones in a snap. I rubbed my hands together in anticipation, nodding.

"I would rather not join your team."

Aaand my dream fell apart. "Sorry, what?"

He got up and paced. "Sorry, Motor, but I just can't! There's too much risk; if the Dark Ones put up a bounty on us . . ." A look of shock appeared on his face. "My Arch, I forgot!" he said, dashing to his bunk, flipping over his pillow, and pressing a button. Steel blinds, like the ones used when mall stores closed, came down over the door and windows. Silver wiped his forehead, breathing a sigh of relief.

"*Now* that nobody can see us, I will continue. If a rich kid like me, a hero of Vaal like you, a fighter like Neon, a smart kid like Yosh, and well, Omalic, get captured, we're doomed! I just can't risk your lives."

I understood. Taking a second to take it all in, I looked at him. "Okay, gotcha. You think you'll put us in danger. Well, okay then! See you later, Sil-*ver!*" I said, slamming the door.

My first thought after being in the hall was, *Why the heck had I done that?* I knew what he meant, but it couldn't be that bad. Sure I'd been knocked out a few times, sure I'd almost gotten killed in a monster spawner, sure I fell for the oldest trick in the book with Stewie. Oh. *Now* I saw his point.

I started to regret my actions. But maybe he would forgive me later. Or maybe he would just say no and go up against us. But before I could think anymore, I heard metal being crunched from the room where I had left. I pulled out my sword and barged into Silver's dorm to see what was in there.

I saw the metal window blinds bitten in half and a weird, small Dark One with the head of a shark and the lower body of a human, only a few inches tall, grabbing onto Silver's head and riding him like a rodeo bull.

I was about to stab it, but it was too close to Silver's head. Grabbing the Dark One and putting it down was out of the question; those teeth were razor sharp. But I decided that there was a way to both help Silver and kill the shark creature.

I put my arms out and yelled to the creature. "Hey chum-face, snack on this instead!"

It immediately stopped riding Silver and paused to look over at a delicious, lean meat hero. Silver noticed what was happening. He yelled out, "Don't do it, Motor!"

But the shark had already decided it was time for dinner and leapt toward me. As I saw his white teeth, I forced my hand with the sword right in front of me, and the shark snacked on a diamond sword, instantly disintegrating into smoke. The bad news . . . it left a smell of dead fish in the room.

Silver stood there, awestruck. After a minute, though, he came back to the world.

"Motor, that was amazing! Sorry about doubting you earlier, it's just—"

I put a hand on his shoulder. "It's okay, I understand."

He stood up and coughed. "So, is . . . is that offer still open?"

I smiled and nodded. We shook hands to seal the deal and Silver did a fist pump.

"Yes, I get to join the team! Will we battle bad guys every day, and get to . . ." He trailed off into his own little heroic world. Meanwhile, I looked down to where the shark had been and found something interesting. It was a weird colored fabric. I cleaned it off and picked it up. I held a rainbow hair bow. It smelled familiar. Like a forest. Then, it hit me.

Silver noticed what I was staring at. He came over, looking in interest. "What's that?" he asked.

I was too stunned to answer. It couldn't be right. It couldn't be possible. There was no way . . .

I ran out of the room, but before slamming the door behind me, I turned around. "Meet in the forest in an hour. And tell Neon, Omalic, and Yosh. We've all got something to discuss."

Chapter 17
Now You See Us...

I sat in the forest clearing with Furry's book in my lap. Sitting around me were Neon, Omalic, Yosh, Silver, and floating Whiteisa. It was sunnier in the clearing and smelled like fresh pine, but it didn't help lighten the mood. I had spent the past hour deciphering and deciding what to do. And after that hour, I had one last resort, and it wasn't a great choice.

I cleared my throat and spoke. "I have gathered you all here to tell you of something horrible. It's about Furry and Shiro. I think . . ." I cleared a lump out of my throat. "I think they are in danger."

Everyone gasped, especially Neon.

"I know this because one, they haven't written anything in quite a while. Two, when a Dark One infiltrated Silver's room, I found this after it was defeated." I held up the rainbow hair bow. Neon looked pale and started to sweat.

"Third, I had a strange dream about Shiro and Furry swimming, but Shiro was pulled down to the bottom of the water by a harpoon."

Neon covered his mouth and ran over to the bushes.

"Well, what are we supposed to do about all this?" asked Yosh.

I sighed, not believing what I would have to say next. "Guys, we're going to have to leave the Academy."

This drew a huge gasp from everyone. They all started talking among themselves about how much homework we would have and how much trouble we could be in.

"Guys!" I shouted. Every eye turned toward me.

"Does it really matter how much trouble we could be in if we're saving Shiro and Furry's lives? They saved mine, so don't I owe them for that? What can a hero be without being heroic?"

Everybody murmured and shook their heads.

"You know what? Fine!" I said, standing up. "If you guys won't join me, I'm going alone! And if I die, you just have yourselves to thank for this!"

I stormed off into the woods away from them. But before I could leave the clearing, I heard Omalic yell behind me, "Wait!"

I turned around. We all stared at Omalic, who was standing up looking at me with a confident gleam in his eye. "I'm coming with you, Motor." He walked to my side of the clearing, turned around, and crossed his arms.

"You know guys, I can't believe you. You would let your best friend go off on a dangerous mission of his own, where he could die? Well, you can add me to that death list because I'm going with him!"

We were silent for a while, taking in what Omalic had said. Finally, Neon stood up and crossed over to the other side of the clearing. "You saved my life and finally let me go on an adventure into the world. I do owe you thanks."

Yosh didn't even wait to come over. He ran as soon as possible and turned around with an icy glare to Whiteisa and Silver.

Silver paused, looked up, and walked over to me.

"I was a social outcast who spent all his days playing virtual spleef. All I had for company was a virtual announcer and some robots. But now, I can live a real life full of adventure and friends. And for that, I am risking my butt to save my new friends." He looked over to me and whispered, "Thank you."

Whiteisa was the only one left. He floated up and looked me in the eye. "I've been serving past heroes both here and in my realm for hundreds of years. They've all been unkind, killed everyone in their way, and were real jerks who were full of themselves." He pointed to me. "But not you, Motorthud. I was never free or had adventures of any sort. In fact, the most interesting thing I did was watch a maggot climb into my coffin and rot. The point is that you are a brave hero who is courteous and kind to his allies and frees the innocent. I'm joining you guys."

And with that, he floated over to our side of the woods. I turned around to face those who would risk their lives for me. They were awesome.

"So we agree we're all going, but we're gonna need to somehow be here *and* rescue Furry and Shiro at the same time," said Neon. "Anyone have a bright idea for how we can do that?"

Yosh rocked back and forth on his feet. "Well, there are a few things I've been working on recently."

We listened, desperate to find out what his plan was.

"Well, it's just, y'know, holograms. Nothing much, just basic video and audio needed and we'll be good to go. Although, I'm not sure I have the materials."

"Yes, that'll be two triple-course outputs and five lightning core scanners. Cool, see ya later." Silver hung up his phone. "Got the materials you need. Anything else?"

Yosh stared at him in awe. He blinked a few times, then shut his mouth. "Um . . . right. Okay, Silver, get the stuff ready ASAP. Motor, Omalic, and Neon, go get ready to record voices in the dorm. I'll tell Whiteisa what he needs to do and meet up with you all later. See you in five minutes."

◆　　◆　　◆

After long hours of recording possible answers to questions and conducting poses like standing, walking, brushing teeth, and loads of others, we were all done. Although, there was one problem. We only had enough time to make holograms of Neon, Yosh, Omalic, and I. Silver would say his father called him to do a commercial after we left and then secretly catch up to us.

But there was still the issue of us, well, not being there. However, Whiteisa still knew how to control beings, objects, and even the holograms. So he would fly into each one, invisibly, when each of us was needed for something specific. He tried one out on me, and I could've sworn there was a mirror between him and me.

Also, there was the question of where we were going and how we would get there. Neon had things under control with a DNA identifier that he found, dusty, in the back of a library. He just collected some slime from Furry's hair bow and had a DNA sample traced of where it came from. In a few minutes, a map popped up on the screen retracing where the goo came from.

When Neon saw it, he made a long whistle. "A heck of a long way, too long for any vehicles' fuel to last," he said. "But anything to save Furry and Shiro." He looked at me, and I nodded encouragingly, assuring him they would be fine and safe. It was ironic really; in the beginning I was the rookie, but I had developed so much that we were equals in almost everything. Just not height. That was disappointing, but I got over it.

And of course, the way we had to get there would be tricky. We couldn't take a jet because it was too loud and would stir up too many questions. We had to go by foot, an agony I had to face like when I first came here. We had to pack heavy for food and only sneaked past the cafeteria staff with so much food by saying we were cramming for a huge test.

With everything set in place, it was time for our amazing disappearing act. We woke up early, before even the weakest of the sun's rays had touched the sky. We had to sneak out through the window via a fire escape ladder. Once we were all down, it automatically retracted back into the room and under the bed, so nobody could find any evidence of our escape.

Except for one thing that I wrote in the book Shiro and Furry sent me. In permanent ink, for anyone who would read it, I wrote an important message:

Dear Reader, In case I do not return from saving Furry and Shiro, please go to Ida and force her to tell you about my past in any way possible. Then, write it all down and put it in this book. Please, just fulfill this dead man's last wish.

Chapter 18
THE HEDGE MAZE OF DEATH

FTER WE HAD LEFT AND I HAD STARED AT THE ACADEMY IN THE rising sun and almost wanted to go back, it wasn't even five minutes until Omalic burst out, "I'm hungry!"

We gave him a blank look. We were on an intense mission to save Furry and Shiro, and he was worrying about being hungry. *Really?* We tossed him a granola bar, which he wolfed down ravenously.

It took us a while before we saw any change in the landscape. From lush, green hills to dark, swampy, Ira Crimex-filled marshes. We had to advance quickly to avoid getting stung. We didn't want another angry Neon. I'm pretty sure nobody would want a furious friend with an iron sword at their throat, either.

At some points, the tracker malfunctioned. Sometimes we ran into hordes of monsters. Sometimes we had to camp in really bad situations, like near a volcano or in a sandstorm. But we kept going to save Shiro and Furry.

A couple days in, though, we came across a lush meadow similar to the one from the Academy. I was about to be angry, thinking that we had just walked across the whole world, but Yosh proved me wrong.

"You would be much more tired, and our food supply would've been depleted days ago," he corrected me.

"Then where are we really?" Silver asked, trying to see up a steep hill ahead of us. He had come by stealth helicopter only a few days earlier.

We ventured up the hill. It was a short walk. At the top, I stopped in my tracks and looked up in awe. There was a giant hedge maze below me, towering about ten feet tall and spanning for a mile in a circle.

Omalic got up and stared, too. "My Arch, that thing's huge," he whispered to himself.

We all gathered and stared at the impossibly huge hedge maze. Who could've made it?

"Guys, the tracker says the monster went through here," Silver pointed out. "It's too wide to go around and there's no way we can climb over that thing without a ladder."

"I can burn a path with this thing easily," Yosh said. He readied his bow and struck it with fire.

Yosh had already released the arrow, which headed toward the leaves. But the leaves didn't move. The arrow merely reflected off them, flying right back at us. We ducked as it flew over and hit a nearby tree, reducing it to ashes.

"Magic. Of course," Yosh said, putting back his weapon. If it was impenetrable and too wide to go around, it looked like we were going to have to go through the maze. The magic scared me, but I was ready.

Everyone else agreed. To save Furry and Shiro, we had to act fast in case they were in huge danger. We split up into groups: Yosh, Omalic, and Silver as one team and Neon and me as the other. We all went into the maze and were soon split up by the leaves.

To move accurately, Silver would have the tracker he was using make a pinging sound into an earpiece Neon wore. The louder it was, the closer they were.

Neon and I only traveled a few feet before we met the first trap. There was a tripwire, easily visible from above. It was at an awkward height, where you could barely walk over or go under it. I hopped over with some difficulty. Neon tripped, and a hole in the ground opened right in front of him. I grabbed his hand before he could fall in, and the hole was covered back up. Before I saved him, I saw hundreds of creepers, ready to explode in the pit below. The maze was clearly set against us.

A bit farther in, I walked and felt the ground drop a little in one step. I heard a hiss, and Neon pulled me back as a mine exploded right where I would've been standing. Afterward, we came across a long path in the maze. When we approached the end, a dispenser came up and shot an arrow. We ducked. It was blocking our path, so we had to keep walking through an arrow storm with our weapons in front of us, deflecting their hits.

At one point, we found Silver, Omalic, and Yosh. We ran over to stick to their tracks, but then a wall of the leaves came up right in front of us. We ran along the route they were trying to take, but the hedges kept blocking our path. It was really getting annoying. I guess we just had to rely on the *ping, ping* in Neon's ear.

And then there were the loose monsters. And boy, were there many. The first was a phoenix, like the one Neon and I originally faced at the Academy. I stood back as Neon sliced, remembering I was allergic to phoenix feather. Then we saw a huge Slime, which looked eerily familiar when it popped into three separate Slimes.

Before Neon sliced the last of it up, I cried out, "Wait!"

He turned around, sword in hand. I crouched above the Slime. It was so small that it couldn't harm me in any way, so I was safe. I stuck out my hand for it to sniff. The Slime, sure enough, sniffed it and started to sort of purr, although it sounded weird when it was through a blob. However, it confirmed my theory.

"Neon!" I said to him. "The maze is a mirror of monsters from our past!" However, he seemed distracted, repeatedly slicing something that his sword deflected off of with a dull *pang* every time he hit it. I walked over to see what he was fighting. Something that looked like a locked gate, blocking our way ahead. It was purple and black like the usual Dark Ones, but this one didn't budge or move. I saw a sign suddenly appear on it, pointed in Neon's direction:

To pass, answer why this fence
You thought would be your very last.

Neon tried slicing at the sign angrily. "Never!" he cried out. He was furious now. He kicked and clawed at the fence until he knelt down, tired from the fight. I thought I heard crying.

I came over, trying to comfort him. "Neon, what's wrong?"

He looked up, red-faced and with tears in his eyes. "I'm not answering that stupid hunk of metal," he said, kicking the fence again.

I could tell it must have been something about his past. Come to think of it, what *was* Neon's past? I was amazed that I hadn't even asked.

"Come on, Neon, it's me. I'm your best friend. Just tell it for me."

It took him a while, but finally he looked up and told me.

"Ida hired me as a servant when I was a boy. I wanted to go on an adventure like her, but I wasn't allowed to until she said the time was right. I . . . I thought I would be trapped there forever as a lonely old man with nothing to do but brush wolves and feed the squids."

There was a creaking sound, and the gate opened behind him. Neon got up, wiping away a tear in his eye. "All right, let's go save Furry and Shiro." His voice was more solid, his movements quicker, and his face turned away. He hurried through the fence, but I wondered how he could get that horrible story out of him with no trouble after he was done. He must've become stronger through training to leave the castle or something. It also explained why it counted as a monster from his past. But after thinking that over, I followed after him.

We saw something else in the maze—Furry and Shiro. We had walked a few minutes past Neon's fence, and there they were, wandering around the maze! Neon shouted to them and bright smiles lit up their faces.

They ran over to us. But before they could reach us, they started to sink into lava puddles. The temperature in the maze suddenly got about twenty degrees hotter. I then realized what was happening.

Neon clung to a branch of a strong hedge, trying to grab Furry to pull her up. I quickly threw my sword in a boomerang fashion, cutting through fake Furry's face and turning her into purple and black ashes.

Neon realized what was going on and tried to get back to the side of the expanding lava river I was on. It was spreading quickly and from both directions. We just *had* to be in the corner of the maze at that time. With no branches and no way to get to the top of the hedge, we were doomed.

But then, I felt something in my chest. No, not my heart, something near my chest. Something moving. I reached in and found the amber Silverquick gave me. The bees inside were buzzing rapidly, and I knew what to do. I threw the amber against the ground, and the bees formed into a thick, floating platform. We hopped on, and the bees (stinger side facing toward the ground) flew us over and around several corners, finally depositing us at a huge clearing where the hedges ended.

It was surrounded by trees, and any light was filtered out by leaves overhead. There was an opening into the light on the other side of the clearing. I made it to that point and was met with an invisible wall. Neon tried running back, but a wall was there, too. Then, it got even darker.

A black and purple Ida emerged from the ground like it was water. She looked up at us, her eyes a menacing, soul-piercing red. She smiled with a creepy glint in her eye.

"This is the last test," she chanted. Her voice was as dark and creepy as the oracle wolf's. "To advance, you must face this challenge." A book suddenly was in her hands. She threw it across the clearing to me, and I caught it. It was cold as ice and holding it, I heard spirits moaning in agony.

"This book contains your past," the dark version of Ida said, "as well as your future. If you read it, you can live a peaceful life and join the Dark Ones. Or, if you choose not to, then you and your friends will most certainly die by the challenges ahead. Your choice, *hero*."

I looked to Neon, in fear of losing him. But he was standing still, not breathing or blinking. I heard nothing around me. The lighting was the same. She must have frozen time! At least she left me enough time to make my choice.

What was I thinking? Of course, I had to deny and fight her!

But still . . . what was my past? And what was Neon's past? Why didn't he tell me? What kind of friend keeps secrets like that?

An answer came across in my mind: *Someone who has experienced many hardships in youth. Someone who is pure of heart and has a tragic story to help them keep fighting. And you have it, too. You may not know it, but the time will come. And when that time comes, you will be ready. And you will know.*

My thoughts were interrupted by Dark Ida, who looked like she had a migraine.

"Quit it! Just quit it now!" she screamed. "Archlinder, leave now!"

She looked to me in desperation. "Just join us! Please! Before—"

"No. I won't look," I said.

She emitted a banshee scream and ignited in sudden fire. She sank back into the ground, engulfed in flames and screaming in agony, and I felt time start to flow again. Neon looked over to me.

"Dude, you look like you just saw a ghost! You okay?"

I smiled, knowing he wouldn't understand, but that he was a friend.

"Nothing, just thinking a bit." At that moment, we heard a rustling behind us. I readied my sword, but Silver, Omalic, and Yosh came running through. Their clothes were torn and their hair singed in some places. They looked like they had been struck by lightning.

But Silver didn't seem to mind. He had a huge smile on his face. He pointed to the other side of the clearing, tracker in hand. "Come on, guys, this way!" He charged past us, and we ran after him, stepping carefully to avoid possible traps.

We burst into light and realized we were out of the hedge maze of doom. But Silver wasn't done running. He continued a few hundred feet until we saw something different from the landscape.

It looked like the rest of the small hills and clouds, but nothing was moving. Trees nearby blew with the wind, but there was one section where time didn't seem to flow. The clouds didn't move, birds didn't fly, leaves didn't rustle. It was strange.

I advanced, sword pointed out. Silver checked his scanner. "It says the goop is traced back here, but only to a spot a little ahead. But it's just a hill."

I poked my sword outward. Part of it disappeared from view. I drew it back to me, and it was back. Uh-oh.

"Silver, that's not just a hill," I warned.

Chapter 19
THE WHEREABOUTS

"SO WHAT ARE YOU SAYING?" SILVER ASKED.

"I'm saying that area just isn't normal!" I exclaimed, pointing to the place where my sword went invisible and came back. "It could be frozen in time, like when I was talking to Ida!"

Neon gave me a strange look. "You talked to Ida?"

I couldn't tell Neon what I saw. He would be shocked if I doubted the good side for even a second.

"That's not important. What does the scanner say, Omalic?" I asked, desperate to not tell what just happened. Even I wasn't 100 percent sure it had occurred.

Omalic checked the scanner. "It says here the entire maze surrounds this one place. It would make sense that those defenses are protecting something important. Otherwise, it's like putting a fence around a random spot of sand in the desert."

Silver took it in. "All right, but how do you suppose we go in?"

Yosh suddenly had an idea. "We could stick Motor's head in."

"What?" I exclaimed. "Why would you shove my head into a potential black hole?" They were out of their minds.

"If your sword could stand it, so could you," Neon assured me. Great. He made some sense, but just barely enough to have me stick my head into yet another potential death trap.

I crawled on my stomach toward the land without time. Omalic and Neon held down my ankles to make sure I didn't get pulled in or fall into whatever was behind there. In case that failed, Silver and Yosh had their weapons ready for potential monsters.

I could see the grass not blowing in the breeze right in front of my face. I was facing the fake area. I could just stick my head in and we could go home. That is, if Furry and Shiro were right there. I concentrated on saving them and stuck my head in.

The grass, bright sun, and clouds were gone. It was much hotter and darker. The red ground was as hard as stone. I was in an entire cave of it, spanning for miles. There were lakes of lava almost everywhere, except for the one spot right in front of me. There, made of black obsidian, was a gigantic castle. Unfriendly walls easily over twice as high as the maze. I didn't have to see it to know that nothing could go right in there. I couldn't take the sight of it; I felt like I was about to die. Despite the hot environment, I felt deathly cold inside.

I pulled out, gasping for air. All four of my friends came to my side, asking me questions.

"What was in there?" "Is it safe?" "Does it have food?"

All I answered was, "We need to go in." I had felt something there, a very dark presence. And where dark presences are, captives are bound to be.

But we had to get ready. Silver spent all night drawing schematics for the raid based on what I told him. Yosh and Neon spent all night thinking of what could go wrong and trying to make sure it wouldn't happen. Omalic worked hard to try and repair our swords to their maximum capabilities. Meanwhile, I fought all night. To get strong and ready. Creepers, spiders, zombies—all were easy matches for me. But I still didn't know if I was ready.

But deep in the night, when we were, by chance, all in a makeshift tent, we heard something. I poked my head out and signaled for the others to be quiet. I saw a purple-and-black, six-foot-tall Dark One slug. I was about to lunge when I saw a Dark One hawk twice the slug's size. Then came more and more Dark Ones, until the only way I could've gotten them all was to drop a nuclear bomb on them.

Omalic and the others saw all the Dark Ones just standing there. They were clearly waiting for something. Then, an echoing bell rang a deep tone. The Dark Ones filed one by one into the dark castle. None remained outside.

I turned around to face the others. "We have to move, now."

They freaked out. "Motor, are you nuts?"

"We could be killed!"

"I'd rather go back into the maze!"

"Guys, there's a huge meeting in there! Their guards will be down, and we could give a surprise attack! Plus, we could sneak in and rescue Furry and Shiro!"

Slowly, they agreed, but mainly for sneaking Furry and Shiro out. We tiptoed out of the tent and to the spot where it still looked like day. I hesitantly poked my head in after what happened the last time. I was greeted, yet again, with the strange cavern and extreme heat and lava. Weird, glowing stones allowed me to see, but just barely.

Neon came in right after, awestruck. "It's practically radiating evil," he said, looking up at the obsidian. Silver and Yosh followed, not saying a thing, but with mouths hanging open in awe. Omalic came in last, so amazed he only said, "It's so hot in here."

We looked around and saw that the only guards were grotesque, mutated pigs with golden swords. Some of the swords had red stains on them. We sneaked past them too quickly to figure out what they were. Luckily for us, the door was open, allowing us to go in without making a racket.

There was a grand hallway with a chandelier of the glowing stone and the weird rocks that made up the ground, which were on fire. They also had several brick creations scattered throughout the hallway. I hated to admit it, but the Dark Ones were pretty good interior designers.

There were three passageways; one to the left that led onto mossy stones, one to the right that led to quicksand and some sort of plant, and one in the middle that led to a room made of bricks. I sensed the Dark Ones gathered here.

"Let's go through the mossy one," Neon suggested. "Seems like a dungeon, which is where prisoners are usually kept."

We were interrupted by two Dark Ones leading people in chains to the mossy path, supporting Neon's point. We kept behind a narrow wall, and they didn't notice.

Silver and Yosh suggested we go through to the quicksand hall because Shiro and Furry might've escaped and hidden in there. Omalic and I pointed out they could be in the brick room as prisoners put on display to be executed or something.

While silently bickering, we heard an explosion, then several more, and saw a dead Dark One fly out of the quicksand side. We unanimously decided not to go that way. That left the main hall and Neon's choice.

"Don't go that way. Why would they be in there? Prisoners belong in dungeons!" Neon said. We argued for about eleven minutes until I stormed down to the middle hall to save Furry and Shiro myself. But then, I saw the room was filled with Dark

Ones, from mice only a few inches tall to dragons that could barely have fit through the castle's front door.

I scampered back and told them how bad an idea it was to go charging in there. Apparently, we were going through the mossy hallway.

We entered a long and dark hallway, brightened with a few torches. As we walked, I heard moaning as we went deeper. Then we saw a jail cell. It contained a mattress full of flies, a rusted canteen, and a skeleton covered in cobwebs. Apparently, the Dark Ones didn't allow parole to inmates.

A few more popped up here and there, until we saw one occupied by someone who wasn't missing skin. It was a six foot guy, stomach caving in, wearing rags, and with eyes pushed into the back of his face. He was banging on the jail bars, trying to get attention for a guard that wasn't coming back.

When he saw our torch light, he quickly started shouting and beckoning us over. He was ecstatic for freedom. We came over, and he looked at us like we were heroes.

"Thanks, I hoped someone would come and free me! Just please let me out!"

I looked at the rusty cage bars. I drew my sword and sliced through them like butter. He jumped out, whooping and hollering with happiness.

"You're welcome," I said in response to his odd thanks. "Now, who are you?"

He smiled. "Oh, I'm Yohans! Thank you so much for letting me out!" he said, shaking my hand.

Neon raised an eyebrow. "Wait, wasn't that the name of—"

I didn't hear the rest of what he said because I was thrown on the ground, and my arms and legs were tied together with rope by Yohans.

He jumped onto the others as quickly and did the same. When Yohans got to Neon, Neon tried to deflect him with his sword, but it was quickly knocked out of his hands, and Neon was on the ground.

Yohans resumed the conversation. "Yes, I am Yohans! And that *was* the name of the notorious murderer put to execution for his crimes. But now, it's Dark One Yohans, thanks to you idiots!" he said, twirling the rope around in his hands.

He took his head and peeled it off, revealing the head of a purple-and-black chameleon. He was almost as tall as I was. He removed the rest of his outfit, showing a black military jacket. He also slid an invisible cover off his now visible tail, which explained how he knocked the weapons away from us.

Two of the zombie pig guards, more humanoid and buff than the ones at the door, came down the passage and right behind Yohans, awaiting further order.

"Knock them out. I'll be in the spa if you need me," he said with satisfaction and walked away with a smile on his face. The pig guards came over, raised their swords, and struck us down. I was out cold.

Now, I can admit I've blacked out my fair share of times, but I think because of those injuries, it explained the vision I had after the blow in the dark castle.

I was in a garden with beautifully decorated stone sculptures like birdbaths, benches, arbors, and tables. Someone dressed in a long black robe that hid his body was sipping tea in an intricately decorated little teacup and kept looking over to a certain area. He was waiting for someone to arrive.

Just then, an explosion shook the beautiful structures, and I saw animals running to the spot where it occurred. The person then set down the tea and sprinted off to investigate where the animals were going.

There were more explosions, and the garden faded. I woke up, rubbing a hand on a recent bruise on my head. I was in what seemed to be the same hall we were in before, but the ceiling was lower, there was a constant crashing coming from above, and the hallway was shorter and curved. It also smelled like rotten fish, or something that had died down there. Possibly, a mixture of both.

I saw Neon in front of me at some bars dividing us from the curving hallway, rattling his hand back and forth. His weapons were gone. I checked my back, and sure enough, so were mine. Yosh, Omalic, and Silver were laid out behind me in an unconscious pile.

I scooted toward Neon. Without turning his head, he said, "So you're awake." He stood up from his kneeled position and turned around. His face had some cuts, as did his pants and shirt. I checked behind me to make sure the others weren't awake. They were still knocked out. It was time for me to ask.

"So, Neon. Back in the maze . . . what was that about your past?"

He looked down. "Well, it's not something I would mention in a regular conversation," he said, rubbing his neck at the discomfort of it all.

"Come on, man, I can help you out. I need to know." I noticed how harsh and rude my request sounded. He didn't respond for a while. He turned toward the bars and ran his hand against them for a while, not saying a word. Then, a few minutes later, he stopped, sighed, and spoke while still facing the hallway.

"July 12, 2184. I was only four years old. I lived in a small town. Duraheim. Everyone knew each other's name, and the days were always good, even in rain. But then, there was that one day.

"I came home after preschool. I was ready for some juice, but when I came in the house, I saw my mom pressed against the wall, eyes bugging out, while a woman had what seemed to be a stick against her throat. She had a long cape and was dressed in black and gray. The woman then noticed me and put her stick down at her side. She turned toward my mother again. 'Remember, eleven by tonight. I need your word.' She then stormed out.

"My mother was in tears. I tried comforting her, but she told me to go to my room. And when my dad came home from work, I heard them both talk about it like they were in grave danger."

I started to think this person was a real villain, but I let Neon continue with his story.

"I remember staying up for hours on end that night, until exactly eleven p.m. to see what would happen. There was a large smash and screams. I looked out my window and saw a really big monster. Purple and black, but it looked like a crocodile. He was several stories tall and wide and floated his way past buildings. Especially scarier was the huge Dark One army following right behind him. With a snap of his fingers, lights exploded. With another, a man was thrown far into the distance.

"My parents saw what was going on and took me outside, and we went as fast as we could into my family's jet. But the beast saw what was happening and snapped his fingers right as we had left the neighborhood limits. The engine exploded. I remembered spinning metal and fire. Then a very hard impact on the ground.

"I was barely alive; crawling for my life as far as my arms could take my body. Then I saw my parents. Blood mixed with glass and the stench of death. But while I was taking that nanosecond mourning them, the creature saw me and snapped a beam of pure darkness heading my way from his jaws. I closed my eyes and was ready to join my parents.

"But there was a bright blue light. I looked up and saw the woman who was in my kitchen only hours ago. She withdrew enchanted arrows and let them fly. And they impacted, but the creature seemed undaunted.

"He put his arms out and smashed them into the ground, sending a huge earthquake our way. I only escaped after the woman realized this was something even she couldn't beat and threw her cape around us. Then, I was in a weird state of being and not being. The light, sound, and heat were different.

"It was a beach. Daytime. Rolling waves, sun in sky, but I had no idea what was going on. I'd just seen a creature destroy my town, break both my legs, and kill my parents. And then, the woman I thought was a threat saved my life.

"I looked into the distance and saw an obsidian tower far across the waves on an island of sand and grass. She said this was my new home. She had also said her name was Ida."

I was shocked. "So Ida threatened your parents but saved your life? But how . . . what the . . . why the . . . ?" I was at a huge loss for words.

"That's what I thought," Neon continued. "And you heard the story after that. I worked for her in exchange for food and a place to live, then you came and I went on an adventure. Not turning out to be a good one, though. It might end soon," he said, glancing around our cell.

"But why did you want to go on an adventure anyway? After all, you just nearly died!"

He shrugged. "True, but that beast destroyed my town, my parents, and what I knew of my life. I wanted to avenge everything I knew to kill it. And to do that, I had to train and get stronger. I heard of the Academy and asked Ida. And you know . . . you, the Academy, now this. But it doesn't look like I'll be doing much in here. I sometimes even think that it would've been better to have died right there."

He sighed. Suddenly, I heard a different sound. Like the jingling of keys. A door opened in front of our cell and blinded us with harsh electric lights. A voice of what seemed to be a Dark-One grunt went through the hall.

"Come on, fresh meat, let's move!" He looked like a two-foot-tall bat in overalls and a trucker's hat, but I didn't say anything because of the sharp dagger by his side. He grabbed a key and unlocked our door. He got Omalic, Yosh, and Silver up by knocking them on the head with the blunt end of his weapon. He connected us together with some old-style handcuffs that were metal and chained our hands together. He led us down the hall to the door and opened it, emitting a blinding light.

He shut the door behind us, and I registered my surroundings: a giant coliseum with fifteen-foot metal walls separating the dirt pit we were in from the stands where all the monsters we saw earlier were. The stands were full, and the monsters were booing, throwing junk and sometimes even knives at us.

There were two doors on the sides of the ring: the small seven-foot one we came out of and a huge metal door on the side opposite us. There was also a floating announcer's booth only two feet away from touching the forty-foot-high ceiling. I also saw some dried blood on the ground and knew the bat was right: we were fresh meat.

The announcer's voice, high-pitched and scratchy, played over the arena. The monsters didn't seem to mind, but my eardrums felt like they were being stabbed.

"Well, it seems our annual Kill for the Will Wrestling

Tournament has had an interruption but a worthwhile one. Monsters of all species, I give you the hero of Vaal!"

A spotlight slid over me, blinding me yet again. I held an arm up to shield my eyes, only making me look more comical to the huge monsters above. They laughed so hard that some couldn't even breathe. The announcer's voice then came back on.

"Yes, what a loser, folks! And among his worthless friends are, as we all know, the son of GoldenSneak's creator who developed Dark One traps, Silverstealth!"

A huge collection of insults and hissing erupted from the audience.

"But now, they will be subdued by the decade champion, the Dark!"

Cheers and whoops came from every monster's mouth at the words of the winner. But the Dark? Wasn't it usually Dark Ones? Then I realized I had that feeling in my gut again, like when I felt Laavacan's power. Only this time, it was about ten times stronger and dragged me down at least twelve times as much. This could *not* be good.

Spotlights crowded around the door in front of us while everyone near the ring scurried away. A loud *bang* of metal was heard, and a fist-shaped indentation appeared in the door. Then again and again. The door burst open off of its hinges, revealing the most powerful villain I'd ever seen.

Now, to imagine the Dark, imagine this. A giant cow skull like you find in the desert, on top of a suit of armor, diamond- and iron-fused, pulled together by skeletal hands with connecting purplish mist that also flowed out of the eyes and nose of the skull. Also, he was menacingly holding a bullwhip that had a barbed, electric end. Oh, did I mention that it was at least thirty feet tall and drenched in blood?

Blood covered the suit of armor in many places, but the skull was bleached white, like it had been dead but preserved for a long time. Also, if that wasn't bad enough, it spoke in an echoing, evil, confident voice.

The Dark tapped an area below its horn, where a tiny headset was.

"Monsters and Dark Ones!" the Dark acknowledged, his scary voice echoing off the walls before it left the room. "I have come here to slay traitors and the good, but it appears we have a surprise guest."

The Dark said "guest" like he was amused. I think I saw him crack a smile between his ancient jaws.

"I will slay them all, from this so-called hero to the weakest of his disordered pack!"

The crowd cheered with excitement. Silver was about to protest, if the dragon in the front row wasn't looking at him so menacingly.

"But I do believe in a fair fight." He called to several giant purple-and-black rats in electrician outfits. "Give them their weapons!" They scurried off, then sprinted back and threw a chest over the stands. It landed at our feet, full of our stuff.

Silver withdrew a combination iron-and-gold sword, which I had never seen before. He seemed to have money all over the place! Omalic grabbed his original bow and arrow. Yosh got the sharpest iron sword he could find, and Neon got his silver ax, a weapon I hadn't seen him use in a while, either. Finally, I withdrew my diamond sword. I balanced it out to see if it wasn't messed with. It was fine, but it felt warmer somehow.

We turned back around to the Dark, who was practicing his whip on nearby targets, reducing them to ashes. We were going to be prematurely cremated.

"Ready to die, eh?" he asked. He looked up to the announcer's booth, waiting for a signal. He looked at us, flexing his whipping arm.

"Ready?" The announcer creaked. I tossed my sword, readying it for the suit of metal-covered mist.

"Set?" Neon did a few practice swings nearby. The Dark bared his teeth.

"*Kill!*"

Since we were all bunched together, the Dark naturally struck there first. We leapt out of the way in time in separate directions, but even from so far away, I felt that thing's power. It was like a generator for New Kobol on steroids electrocuting you if you got hit. I tried running through the Dark's legs, but he wasn't as dumb as some of the other enemies I had faced. When I was between the legs, he quickly snapped them together as I jumped away. The force of the snapping blew me back against the cement wall.

Yosh launched a round of arrows, which the Dark swept aside with a hand. The arrows swept into the audience, on fire, causing the Dark Ones in the stands to scatter. Silver threw his sword at the Dark, causing an impression to appear in the chest plate. Not a breakthrough, though.

Neon swung his ax through a space in the armor between the Dark's foot and leg, but it was just mist and caused damage only to Neon, who the Dark noticed and kicked back into a wall. While the Dark was distracted, I tried to climb up the wall to the stands and jumped off onto the Dark's back.

I climbed up to his neck and had just the space to put my sword right in his eye. But since it was a skull, he felt no damage. Omalic didn't see me behind the head and fired a shot, which missed the Dark's skull and grazed off a part of my armor, drawing some of my blood in the process.

The Dark threw his head forward, sending me flying near a wall. I leaned backward to slow down and fell right before it. He also whipped near the area where I would've crashed, causing sparks to fly and that part of the concrete to explode.

Omalic had tried a few more times to fire, failing. The arrows landed in the crowd, causing a few frightened creepers to explode and Dark Ones to flee the now-burning arena in terror. Yosh had also tried stabbing the Dark in the foot. But, like Neon, he was causing no damage and was nearly killed. However, he was close to being stomped on but held the foot back with the flat side of his sword.

Neon had gotten back up and tried to swat the whip out of the Dark's arm. He only managed to put a few dents in the armor's fingers before he was flung onto the floor.

The Dark picked up Silver in a large hand, smiling to himself. He drew the hand with the whip closer to Silver, about to slowly electrocute him. I jumped, sword in hand, to the spiked end of the whip. I was filled with electricity and pain but managed to knock the whip out of the Dark's surprised hand. He also loosened his grip, letting Silver free.

Yosh also managed to jump out from under the Dark's foot and sliced off part of his horn. But it wasn't a victory; the horn, on the floor, grew purple, misty tendrils and attached itself to the Dark's previously empty tip. The Dark had picked his whip back up. The weapon glowed like it was about to explode, and I saw black mist coming out of his nose, under the angry glance in his eyes and above the angry grimace on his face. He was *furious*.

With his empty hand, he grabbed Omalic and bashed him against the wall, while kicking me out of his way. Omalic slid down, a sickly red trail following him. The bow fell out of his hand and hit the ground with a sharp crack heard all around the room. He heard it and, turning around, balled his fists. He stood there for a moment, breathing heavily with blood running down his face and shirt. He turned his head and spat out a tooth, wiping his mouth right after.

"You," he snorted. "You invaded our lands, established an enterprise of darkness, and killed millions upon millions, including my family. But that . . . oh, you'll pay for that you son of a Blaze!" He jumped onto the Dark's armor with incredible speed. He leapt from one seam of the armor to another, until he was finally at the Dark's head. He pulled back his arm, and shouting, plowed a straight line from the Dark's left eye to a few feet below the start of his jawline.

The Dark roared in pain, grabbing Omalic and throwing him down like a meteor. Then, he charged straight toward us. I was the only one left in his way. He snatched me up and threw me into his mouth. If the judge was still there, that might've been called as an illegal move.

I crouched down and set my sword upright between the top and bottom of his jaws, so he couldn't move his mouth or utter a word. Luckily, I was so far back he couldn't reach in there. Unluckily, I was so far back, if I scooted back anymore, I would fall into his stomach.

Just as my sword was about to bend from the jaw's pressure, Yosh threw a sword he found lying on the ground into the Dark's mouth. I ran over to the weapon and threw it down his throat. He opened his mouth in surprise, allowing me to grab my sword and jump out before he could chomp down.

I saw that Yosh hung onto and stabbed a slit between the hand and arm pieces of the Dark's armor. Omalic, despite his injuries, pounded into small chinks in the armor. Neon jumped up and tried to cleave weak spots in the metal, and

Silver threw his gold-and-iron sword like a boomerang to the Dark's neck line.

The coliseum was burning in various spots as I put my sword in one of them, remembering its enchantment. It burst into flame at the blade, and I ran forward in front of the Dark. I did a quick slide to his left, getting away from his hands that came down where I would've been.

I jumped off the wall onto his back again, reaching the point between his armor and the back of his head. I stabbed down and flames spewed out. His head caught fire, and burned like it was wood. He reached the back of his neck and threw me forward into the wall, while launching his whip at me.

This time he was too strong and fast, so I got a spike through my leg and was shocked with hundreds, if not thousands of volts of electricity. I fell to the floor, clutching the new hole in my leg. I knew what it felt like to be a steak now. Something to check off my appropriately timed bucket list. Blood spread like the Dark's fire. But the fire wasn't hurting him anymore. He had no reaction.

"Silly fool!" he said, his voice booming across the room. "Haven't you realized you should give up? My aura practically steals your enchantments."

I looked down at my sword. The enchanting marks that were previously there had disappeared.

His head blazing, he charged forward at Yosh, who caught fire. He threw down his weapon, and screaming, he stopped, dropped, and rolled. But the Dark saw this coming and hit Yosh with the sharp end of his whip without electricity. Yosh didn't move.

The Dark charged Silver, hitting him with the shocking part of his whip. Silver received more electrical output than I got, probably because of the devices he had all over his body. He stayed as still as Yosh.

Omalic wasn't quick to finish off. He climbed up the armor and onto the Dark's back, reaching his horns and trying to steer him. However, he forgot about the fire and fell off. While he was in midair, he was kicked into the wall, creating a human-sized hole. He tried to crawl up, but then fell.

The Dark's flames were black and purple with adrenaline. He turned toward Neon, giving a smug, evil smile. He charged forward, fist out. Neon couldn't do a thing as the Dark thrust his fist forward, and Neon flew into the stands through the window of a hot dog cart and stopped at the hard stone wall. Dust settled around him.

The only ones moving were the Dark and me.

I struggled to my feet, and we circled each other, facing off. The Dark was tired but could've gone for a few more rounds without a sweat. The hole in my leg made me limp, but I kept circling him. He laughed.

"How could you think you could beat me in the first place? Your friends are dead, you have a chunk missing from your leg, and you're nearly with them now. Why not join us? You are somewhat a worthy ally, though nowhere near my strength."

Anger surged within. He had killed my friends, and I was nearly dead, but I now had more of a reason than ever to finish him off. *You can do it,* I thought. But it wasn't my voice in my head, it was someone else's. It sounded very wise.

But to try finishing this one off, allow me to take the reins, please. I decided I should, after being beaten to near death. It was new and possibly a threat, but I couldn't go on my own any longer. I relinquished control of my body, which got as warm as my sword did at the start of battle.

The strange voice spoke through my mouth to the Dark. *"Dark, feel the wrath of Motorthud and face the power of the light."* I raised my sword. *"For Archlinder!"*

I dashed forward and leapt up, performing expert sword moves like jabs and swipes that I was incapable of doing independently. I flipped all the way to the Dark's head and stuck my sword into his skull, then removed it. Light cracked through the skull and spread through his body, causing more cracks to appear.

He freaked out, filled with rage. "No, this can't be happening! I'm not going! *I'm not going!*"

He went into a fetal position. The room got darker, specifically around him. He jumped up and released a force of darkness that blasted me back into the wall. The Dark made one last taunt.

"Hah!" he laughed. "You think you could possibly stop me, as weak as you are? Fool! You deserve this, you know."

I heard the voice again, as my vision started to blur for the last time.

I'm sorry about that. Come now, let me get you to a better place.

Chapter 20
GARDEN OF THE GOD

FTER BLACKING OUT FOR ABOUT THE SIXTH TIME IN MY JOURNEY, I expected to wake up in a different place. I was right. I was in the same garden I saw when I was knocked out by Yohans earlier. The grass I was lying on felt like a nice carpet.

I looked down and saw the place where the hole in my leg had been was now covered in bandages. The arbors and stone statues I had seen were just ahead, but the mysterious person wasn't there.

I stood up and walked toward the bench that the strange figure had sat on earlier. My leg felt normal. I sat down and looked around, not sure what to do. Everything was bright and a nice emerald green except for the statues, which were actually marble. I saw a glowing tree in the distance made out to be a throne, with many animals around it. Someone sat there, looking at ease.

I sat up a bit to try and take a closer look, when I heard a voice next to me. "I wouldn't do that yet."

I nearly jumped up in fright as I heard the voice in my head from earlier. I turned to my left and saw the same hooded figure, sitting on the bench next to me where it had just been empty. The hood was too far over its head to let me see the face, but I could tell from the calm, deep voice that it was a man speaking. Perhaps a monk?

"I have been waiting for your arrival in this place," he said, gesturing to the trees around him. The robe covered his hand and wrist like it did his head, still giving me no hint as to who he might be.

I looked around. "What is this place, exactly?" I asked. I couldn't tell if this was a realistic dream or a dreamy reality.

"This is the Garden of the God, far away from any living beings. Peaceful, serene, and a nice place for guests. Although, I haven't had many for a while," he said, examining some dust on the bench's arm.

"Away from people? What about them?" I asked, pointing to where I saw the throne. He shook his head.

"There are always exceptions for others. Plus, don't visit them yet. I must talk to you some more first, Motorthud."

Now I was genuinely creeped out. "How did you know my name?"

"Because I know all. Allow me to introduce myself." He reached his hands to his hood and brought it slightly back, revealing a human skull.

"I am Archlinder, Vaalbara's deity."

I jumped back, grabbing my sword. "No way man, you are not the god I know!" He quickly drew his hood back over and shook his hands. "No, no! I'm not a Dark One! I knew I should've waited before revealing myself. Here, have some tea to calm down."

He snapped his fingers, and it seemed that the atoms in the air transformed into a teapot. He adjusted his hands and the tea poured into the teacup in front of me. He then clapped his hands, making the atoms go back into the environment, like the teapot was never there.

He put his hands down and sounded a bit more cheerful. "That proves to you I'm not a Dark One?"

I sat up and got back on the bench, more relaxed. I knew Dark Ones pretty good, and there was no way they could change the structure of molecules around them. Or make tea for guests.

"So how could you live so long?" I asked Arch.

He smiled. "Live? Motor, I have disappeared from your world a long, long time ago. This is just a realm I have created. No violence, destruction, or warfare; just peace. The only way I am still somewhat alive is due to the knowledge of people."

He held out his covered hand and a bright, floating orb appeared. "This is my life essence," he said. It looked a lot like the orbs I got from killing monsters and used in enchanting weapons.

"I have used it to paint this little world," he explained. He waved his hand with the essence inside, making a bunny appear like the teapot did. He opened his hand back up, and the orb was gone.

"The more people believe in me, the more I have of this to make things happen, even in your world. Before, it was all just blank in here. Just me and my robe. Once a 'crazy philosopher' started thinking people would believe in me and there would be hope, people eventually started believing. They generated the essence through praying and believing, giving me power to run things. So I made this realm for myself, and a few little miracles every now and then for your people."

I was confused. "Why can't you just remove all the world's problems?"

"Well, Motor, that essence is limited. A handful of it only made a rabbit, and it takes many handfuls to make a human. Plus, I only get a few per day from believers down below. To save everything, well, put simply, I would die."

But Arch turned back to the original conversation. "I have brought you here so you, the hero of Vaal, wouldn't have died in vain. The Dark would've killed you entirely had I not preserved you."

"Uh . . . thanks?" I said, not sure if he was gloating or had a valid reason to be thanked. "But how did you do that thing where you got inside me?"

I could tell he was smiling. "It was a lot of essence from time to time, but you needed someone to guide you. Now, about the final battle with the Dark. I'm sorry. I should have sent you a signal, told you not to go, but I was too dry on essence to do anything at that point. When I had finally built up enough, you were already at his castle. If you're going to defeat him, you'll need to adventure more and help more people. Although, if you desire even more assistance, spread my word. If more believers join, I can create more essence, and hopefully, all of our combined efforts can generate enough strength to overcome the Dark. That's a pretty tough challenge and will require tons of strength and fortitude, especially with some plagued cities and people."

"So you want me to become a missionary?"

"All that I'm saying is that if we're going to restore peace, everyone will be playing a key role."

I went over what he had told me. "Help a lot of people to save Vaal? No problem! I can start with Shiro and Furry!"

Arch sighed. "Well, not exactly. Come, let's walk."

We got up and came to the edge of the woods into the clearing where the throne was located. Shiro sat on top of the throne in relaxation wearing a dress made with natural colors. A vine laurel sat perfectly balanced on her head. She was surrounded by animals that were looking at her like she was their mother. There was a huge hole in the ground that animals kept leaping out of to see her.

Furry was kneeling in front of her, tears in her eyes. She had cuts, bruises, scrapes, and dirt all over her. The two looked completely different from when I had last seen them.

"Why are they here?" I whispered to Arch, trying to figure out what the heck was going on.

"Well, they both ended up here the way you did, but in a different battle," he explained.

Then, it all clicked. Why I was here, in a nonexistent environment, after a battle. I dragged Arch back to the bench I was at earlier.

"Am I . . ." I choked. "Am I dead?"

Arch sat down and patted me on the back. "What the *me*, Motor? Why would you be here if you were dead? You blacked out, not seeing the light, right? Plus, you can feel everything. The pain in your leg is nonexistent because of the environment's safety. Plus, Shiro and Furry are here for a different reason. Well, the two are here for different reasons from each other."

I remembered something that seemed like years ago. The pit, the animals, the child of Archlinder. "Is Shiro . . . is she a Creator?"

He nodded. "Through only a few ways does someone find out they are, my child. Either someone tells them, or I send them a message. Well, after the battle, let's just say Shiro found out how to control her powers properly a little too late. However, Furry wound up here like you did, so . . ."

I gasped. "So Shiro's gone?"

Arch nodded solemnly.

How could this have happened? One of the people that I knew the best who trained me to be the hero was gone? What had happened to the both of them while I was gone? I almost felt mad at myself for not writing more and nearly blamed myself for Shiro's death.

Arch sighed. I looked over, seeing him glance at Furry and Shiro.

"You know, life is a strange thing," he said, suddenly holding a summoned dandelion. "You just pick it up, play with it for a while, and then whoosh—it's gone." He blew the dandelion, sending spores into the air, which then disappeared. He reached down and picked up a rose.

"But the afterlife is different. It doesn't vanish as quickly." He blew on the rose, and the rose moved slightly but didn't blow away. "However, no matter how beautiful it may seem, it always has its thorns," he said, plucking a few of them out of his robe.

"The point is, you need to always do something with the time you have. The dandelion can spread spores of legends and change easily, but a rose can't. The dandelion can go places, while the rose is stuck here. Motor, be a dandelion. Spread those spores and make sure that the lawn of Vaalbara is free of pesky slugs."

I looked up at him admiringly, thinking about the weirdest metaphor in the world that he had just told me. Then I remembered something.

"Where are Omalic, Yosh, Silver, and Neon?" They hadn't looked very alive when I had last seen them.

Arch looked forward, smiling to himself. "The Dark is not the brightest, thinking your friends were dead. They are in existence near your starting point. However, time and space don't apply to you since you are in the Garden of the God. This isn't the afterlife for sure, just my realm. The other place is different for everyone, filled with deceased others and memories. This is just a house, and the afterlife is a whole other neighborhood."

I nodded, taking it in.

Arch asked a question that came out of nowhere. "May I see your sword?"

I handed it over to him reluctantly. He picked it up and turned it in his hands. He then threw it into the air, where it floated and turned in a circle. His hands danced near it, in all sorts of motions that I couldn't recognize, like they were incantations. He handed it back to me.

"Many hardships, I see, but the sword should now be repaired. Just like when you started. I also removed any Dark Ones' sludge and other foul slimes and stains."

I looked at my blade and saw that the fire aspect had returned. "Thanks. So, what do I do now?" I asked. His lessons were all coming together in a mish-mash.

"Remember what I have said and what you have seen. Remember Furry's remorse. Remember to do something the world will remember. One may find a gift from someone special to help them. But remember in this dangerous journey, any small mistake could have you end up like Shiro over there."

I nodded. "I'll try my best."

He nodded, most likely smiling under the hood. "Now come, walk with me." He shuffled toward where I thought I had seen a cluster of trees but now it was a dirt path. I followed, and soon we approached a place where the sky was blue, birds tweeted happily, and there was a small pond in the middle of the clearing. It looked familiar.

"Yes, this is where I get the essence. It comes through this lake, and I can send out miracles or inspiration. It's a sort of post office of the god. You can come through here, and you will find somewhere you woke up once."

I looked into the water and saw a completely different world, an upside-down one. The sky wasn't reflecting on the water, the sky was on the opposite side of it. There were also mushrooms on the other side, trees growing upside down, and multiple animals defying gravity.

It was an inverted version of Shiro's lake.

But why would he send me here? I looked into the water again and saw sleeping versions of Omalic, Neon, Yosh, and Silver. They looked bruised but fine.

"Now remember my words, Motor. And also recall that even when you think you are, you are never alone. As soon as you return to the world, you should seek out a familiar friend. And remember, do what I said for me. For Vaalbara. For *Shiro*."

I took one look at him and smiled. I looked at the place around me. Isn't this where I wanted to be? Peace, harmony, and not a care in the world? But then again, Arch was right. I was a dandelion, and it was time for me to leave this field and spread my spores elsewhere. That way, Vaalbara could be its own Garden of the God.

I turned around again, looked at him, and jumped feet first into the lake. I felt no water, only time speeding up, resuming rather than staying still. The world turned upside down, and I jumped out of the lake, feet first, onto the grass around it, into Vaal again.

I looked back into the lake, but I didn't see this place on the other side, only Arch and some trees on the other side of the world. He waved to me, then turned away and walked out of sight.

The water rippled and returned to normal water without a different dimension on the other side. Looking down, I also noticed the bandages around my leg. I peeled them off, painlessly revealing no hole or giant blood spot.

I heard a moan and turned to see Neon awake, rubbing his head and yawning. He smacked his lips and looked around. First slowly, then quickly, double-checking everything.

"Am I dead?" he asked me. What else would you assume after you blacked out to a giant demon?

"No, we're at Shiro's lake. I had some . . . help from a friend to get us here. You might know him." He was about to ask who, but Yosh, Omalic, and Silver woke up, asking whether or not they were alive.

When I told them we were at Shiro's lake, I remembered. How could I tell them that she was gone? But how *could* I know, after not seeing her for months and suddenly knowing her well-being? It would seem too strange and creepy. I stopped thinking, but at that moment, Arch popped into my head.

Remember, find a familiar friend. Save Vaalbara. Do it for Shiro.

I nodded to myself. I beckoned to the way I had come so long ago. "Come on, we need to go somewhere."

We ran through the forest, noticing the turquoise blue ocean, the inviting orange sun, and the emerald-green trees. Maybe this is what we could do. Maybe this could be all of Vaal if we just do something. Then, I remembered my first thought.

I awoke in a pristine forest.

It was pristine all right, but could everywhere be, too? The Academy, New Kobol City, even the Dark's headquarters? Maybe we just had to keep our minds to it and persevere. Then we could save the world.

After minutes of running in silence, we came upon a little wood cottage I had seen before, where I had started my journey in the first place. Not pausing, I opened the door and came inside. I suddenly heard a cry of joy from the bedroom.

"Motor! You're here!"

I had a feeling a whole new adventure was about to begin.

About the Author

ANDREW DALY is a 15-year-old author of middle grade/young adult fantasy stories. *Portal of Vaal* is based loosely around his adventures within a Minecraft community server, and more specifically, the people inhabiting it.

Andrew currently lives in Charlotte, North Carolina with his parents and dog Swiffer. He enjoys writing, reading, playing video games, Netflix binge-watching, and zip lining. He started writing *Portal of Vaal* at age 12 as a short story that culminated into a novel.